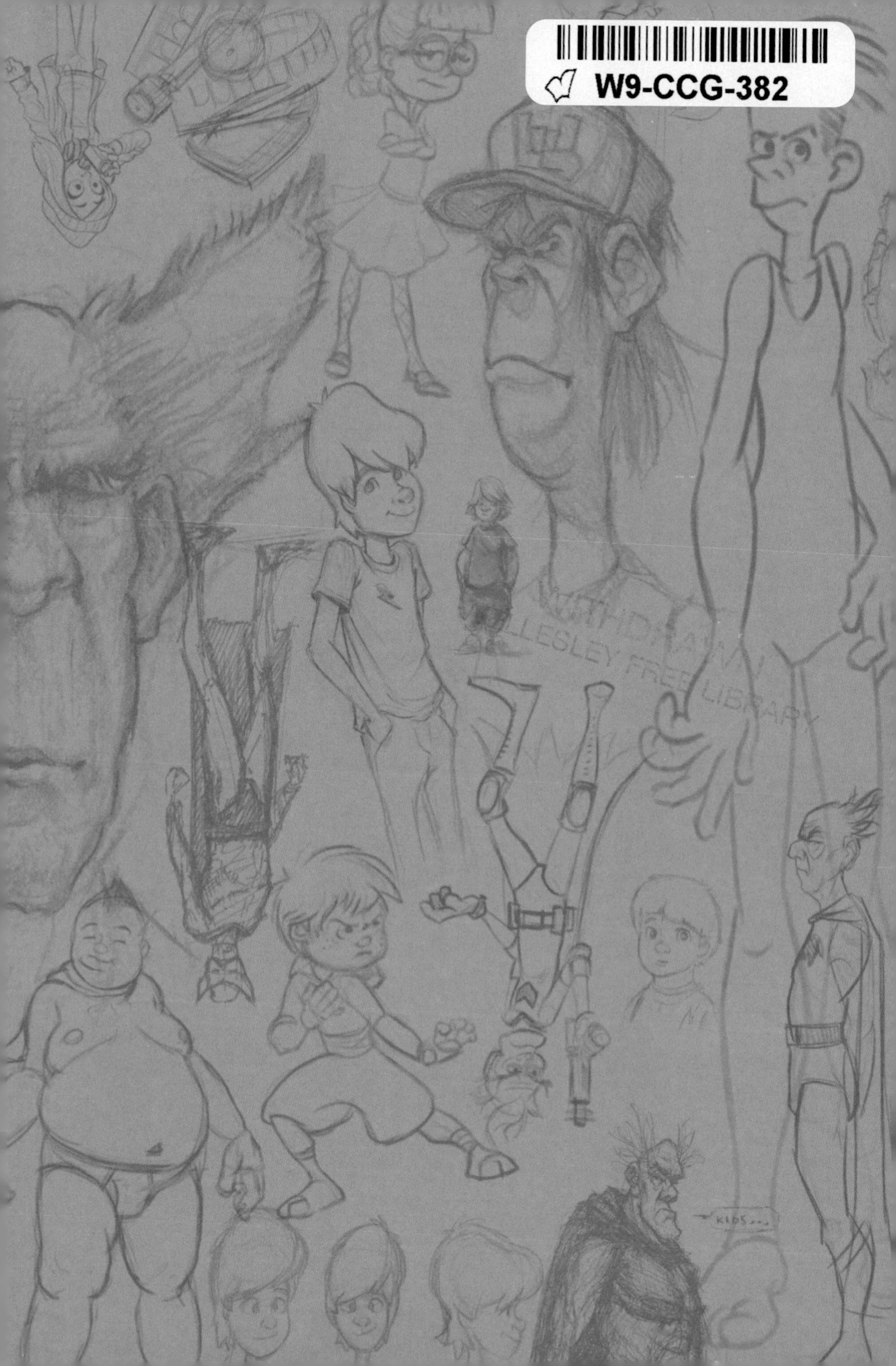
KIDS...

SUPERFAIL

by Max Brunner

Illustrated by Dustin Mackay

RP | KIDS
PHILADELPHIA

Special thanks to Sebastian Kings, Sarah Jaques, Clayton Kober, Lauryn Danae, Kristen Psinakis, Clayton Wood, Christopher Ruiz, and Michael Sanchez.

Running Press Kids
Hachette Book Group
1290 Avenue of the Americas, New York, NY 10104
www.runningpress.com/rpkids
@Running_Press

Printed in China

First Edition: October 2017

Published by Running Press Kids, an imprint of Perseus Books, LLC, a subsidiary of Hachette Book Group, Inc.

The Hachette Speakers Bureau provides a wide range of authors for speaking events. To find out more, go to www.hachettespeakersbureau.com or call (866) 376-6591.

The publisher is not responsible for websites (or their content) that are not owned by the publisher.

Print book cover and interior design by
Frances J. Soo Ping Chow and Dustin Mackay

Library of Congress Control Number: 2016945290

ISBNs: 978-0-7624-6229-2 (hardcover),
978-0-7624-6230-8 (ebook), 978-0-7624-6455-5 (ebook),
978-0-7624-6456-2 (ebook)

1010

10 9 8 7 6 5 4 3 2 1

When my parents find out that I fried the neighbor's cat, they'll probably sentence me to fifteen to life in my room. At least I'll have some muscles when I get out—everyone knows the only thing to do in prison is to lift weights. I'll probably grow a sweet beard, too.

You might be thinking, why don't you just close one eye and fire your good laser? That'll work, right?

I hate my super powers.

Flying at high speed over a city and shooting lasers out of your eyes might sound pretty awesome, but trust me, it's not. Not for me, at least. My super powers are more like a super curse.

This is me trying to use my laser vision.

CAT BURGER →

MY TARGET ↖

Yeah, shooting lasers out of my eyes *would* be a pretty sweet power . . . if I wasn't cross-eyed!

CHAPTER
ONE

ME [A.K.A. MARSHALL]

To anyone who has ever felt "defective"

Wrong!

Turns out eyelids can't stop a high-powered laser. Who knew?

What's worse is even if I don't use my powers, I'm still cross-eyed. I have a pair of sunglasses I wear, and those help hide my eyes, but my teachers won't let me wear them in class.

TAKE OFF THE SHADES, MR. PRESTON. THIS ISN'T THE BEACH.

WHOA! CHECK OUT CRAZY EYES OVER THERE. MAYBE IF I SMACK HIM IN THE HEAD A COUPLE TIMES, I CAN KNOCK THAT GOOGLY EYE BACK INTO PLACE.

I'm not going to lie—if they'd let me wear my glasses, I'd totally sleep through history class. But that's not the point.

And my crossed eye is just the start of my problems. About a year ago, I figured out how to fly. Pretty cool, huh? Not for me. The day I learned how to fly was also the day I learned that I get severe motion sickness.

I really can't fly anywhere unless I want to lose my lunch, which means I don't fly anywhere. Ever. I want to be famous for saving the city, not for dropping barf bombs all over it.

So I have awesome powers that I can never use. See what I mean? I'm cursed.

It doesn't help that I have to deal with a bunch of other problems, like my twin sisters . . . or maybe they're triplets? I'm not really sure. Honestly, I have no idea how many sisters I really have, because at least one of them was born with the power to clone herself.

My mom isn't a big fan of that power.

It's not my favorite, either.

At least *their* power works the way it's supposed to. I'm jealous of my two-year-old sister/sisters. How sad is that?

But I'm way more jealous of the kids at school. Trevor Bretton's a year older than me and he got some sweet powers after a meteor hit his house.

So, his first day back at school was pretty awesome.

A week later, Trevor saved our town from a hurricane created by a mad scientist and was recruited on the spot by the most awesome heroes our city has ever seen—the Superteam. Newscasters called him Superteen and acted like they didn't know his true identity. Seriously? All he did was take off his glasses and put on a cape. Even my sisters knew it was Trevor, and they're only two years old!

That's been my dream for basically my entire life: to save the city, get my picture in the paper, and be recruited to a superhero team. Then I could move into my own place so my sisters couldn't chew all my stuff, and I could finally kill zombies in peace.

But how would I stop a criminal? By barfing on him? Besides, the closest thing to a crime I'd ever seen in our town was my Uncle Doug stealing his neighbor's newspaper.

A GROWN MAN IN CARTOON PAJAMAS. THAT'S THE REAL CRIME!

And the few times I tried to step in to help with something small, I made things worse.

There are only so many pets you can fry before you decide to hang up your cape. That's why I had pretty much given up on the whole becoming-a-superhero dream.

CHAPTER TWO

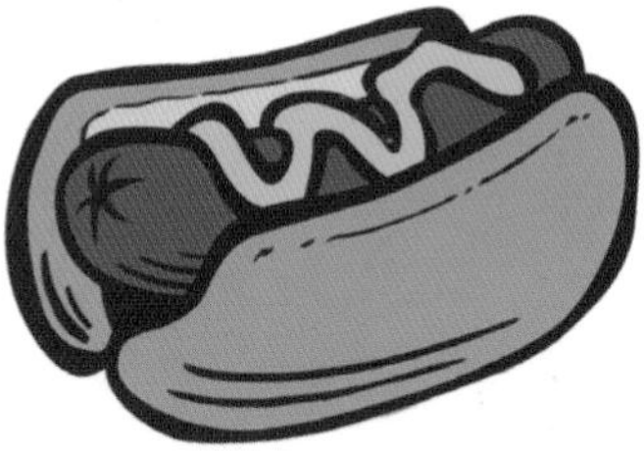

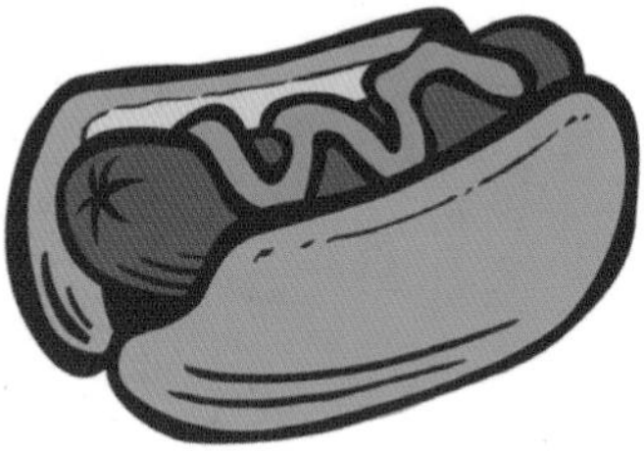

My parents make me pull weeds at my grandma's house every Friday. Most grandmas are sweet old ladies who give candy and silver dollars. All kids have to do to earn treats is let them pinch their cheeks.

Not my grandma.

The old man next door is just as bad. He's always outside watering his garden, but doesn't pay attention to where he's spraying.

Anyway, last Friday I was hauling my grandma's trash cans out to the curb when it happened.

SCREECH!

SMASH

THUMP

SLAM

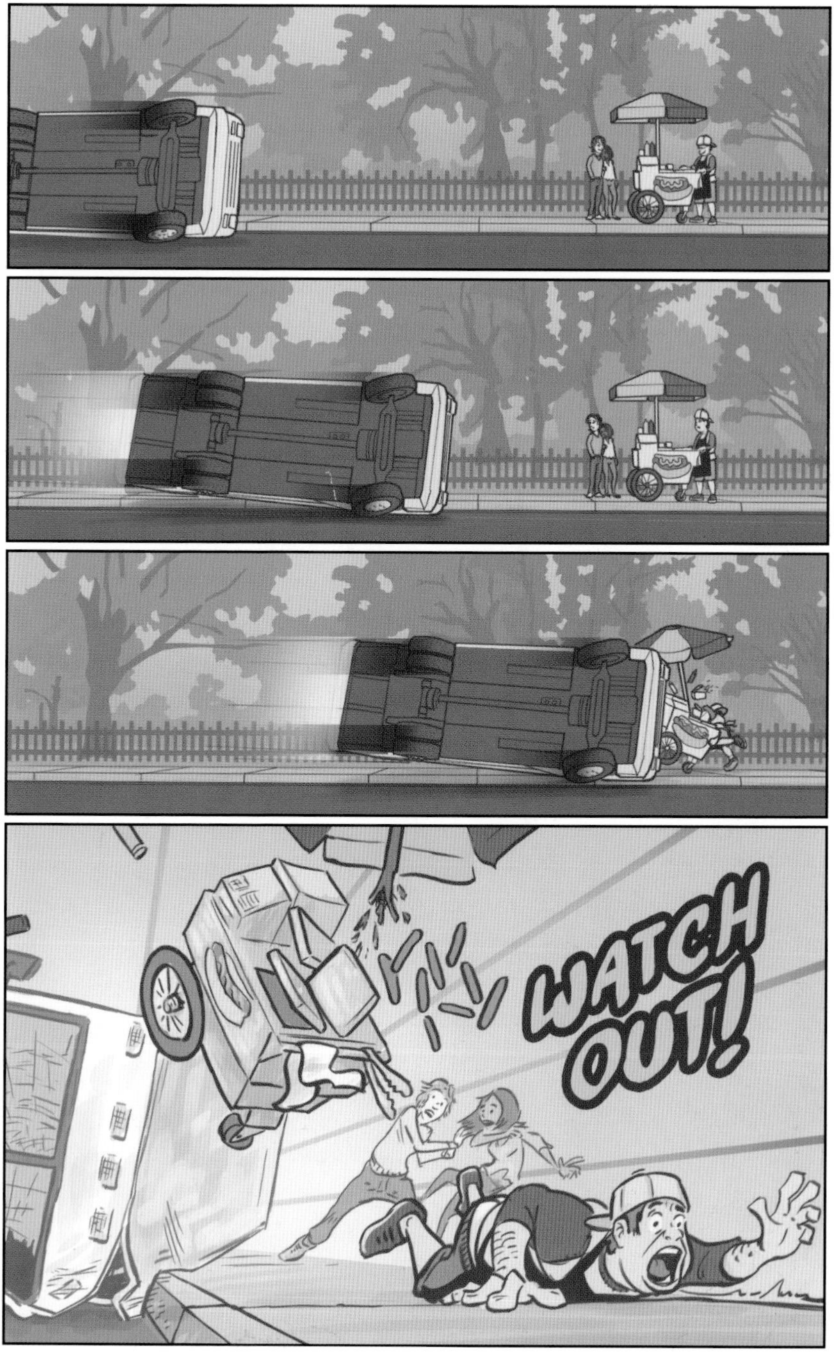
WATCH OUT!

A bunch of guys jumped out of the van. I knew if I tried to blast them, I'd probably end up frying another pet, so I took off in the other direction. Or at least I tried to. Joey, the biggest tattler in school, ratted me out.

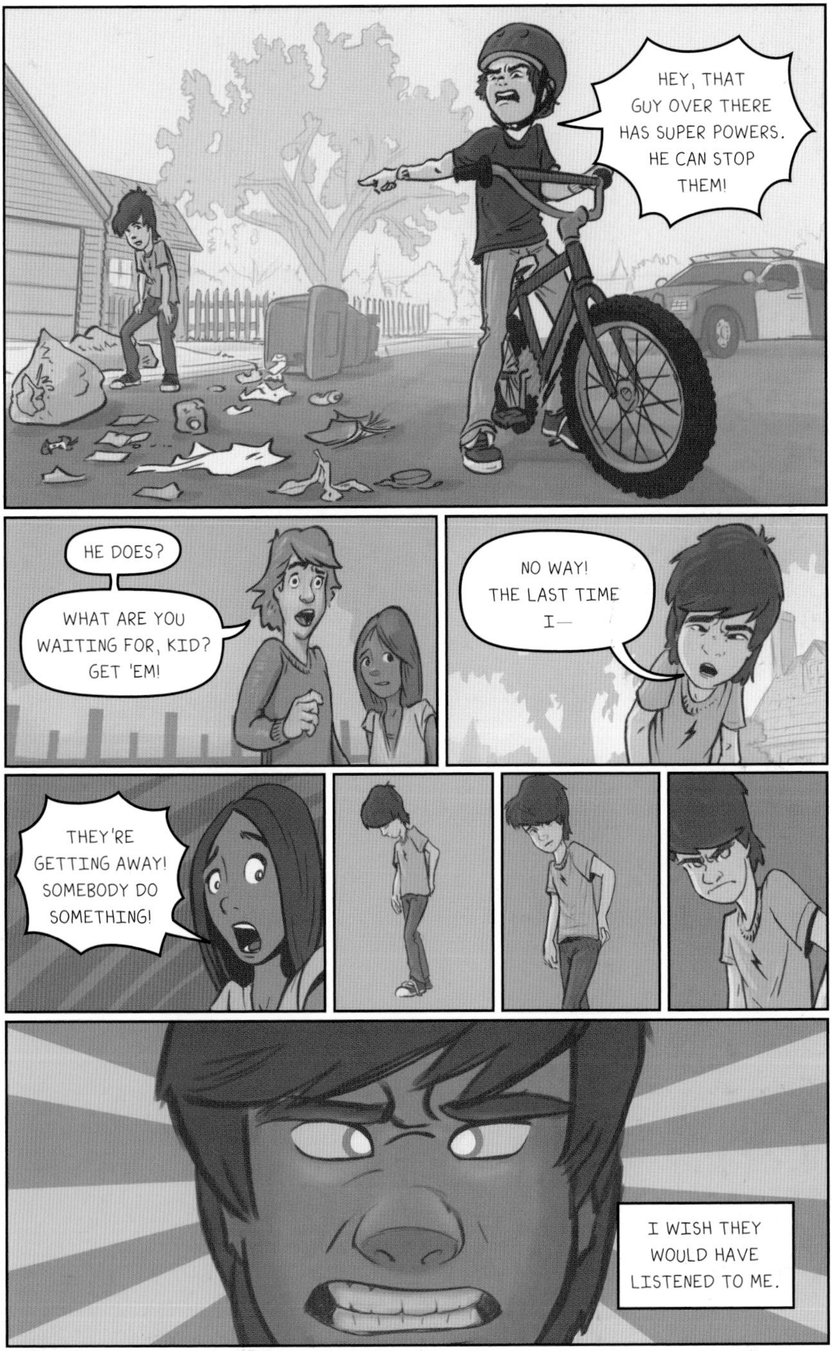
HEY, THAT GUY OVER THERE HAS SUPER POWERS. HE CAN STOP THEM!
HE DOES?
WHAT ARE YOU WAITING FOR, KID? GET 'EM!
NO WAY! THE LAST TIME I—
THEY'RE GETTING AWAY! SOMEBODY DO SOMETHING!
I WISH THEY WOULD HAVE LISTENED TO ME.

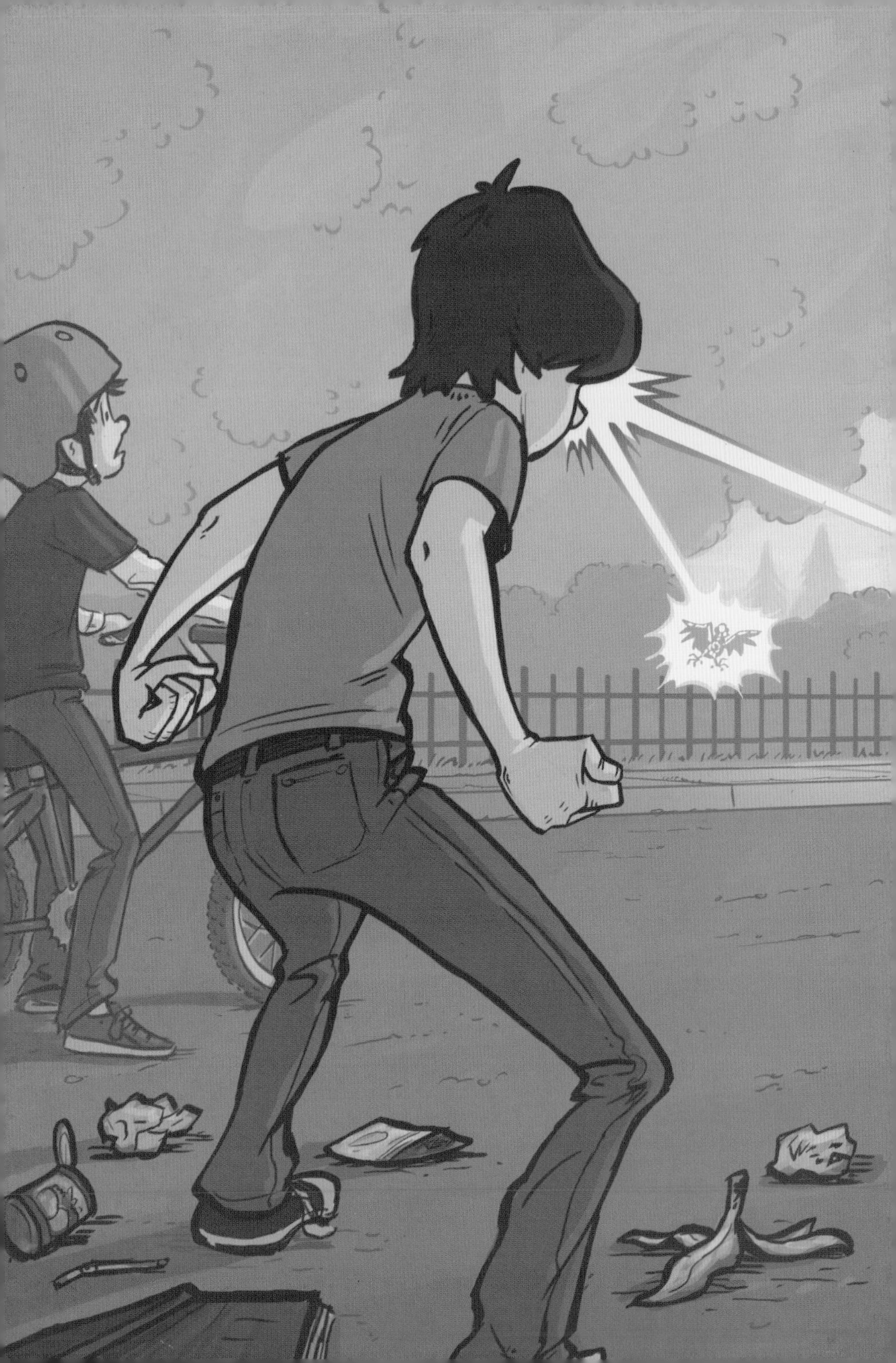

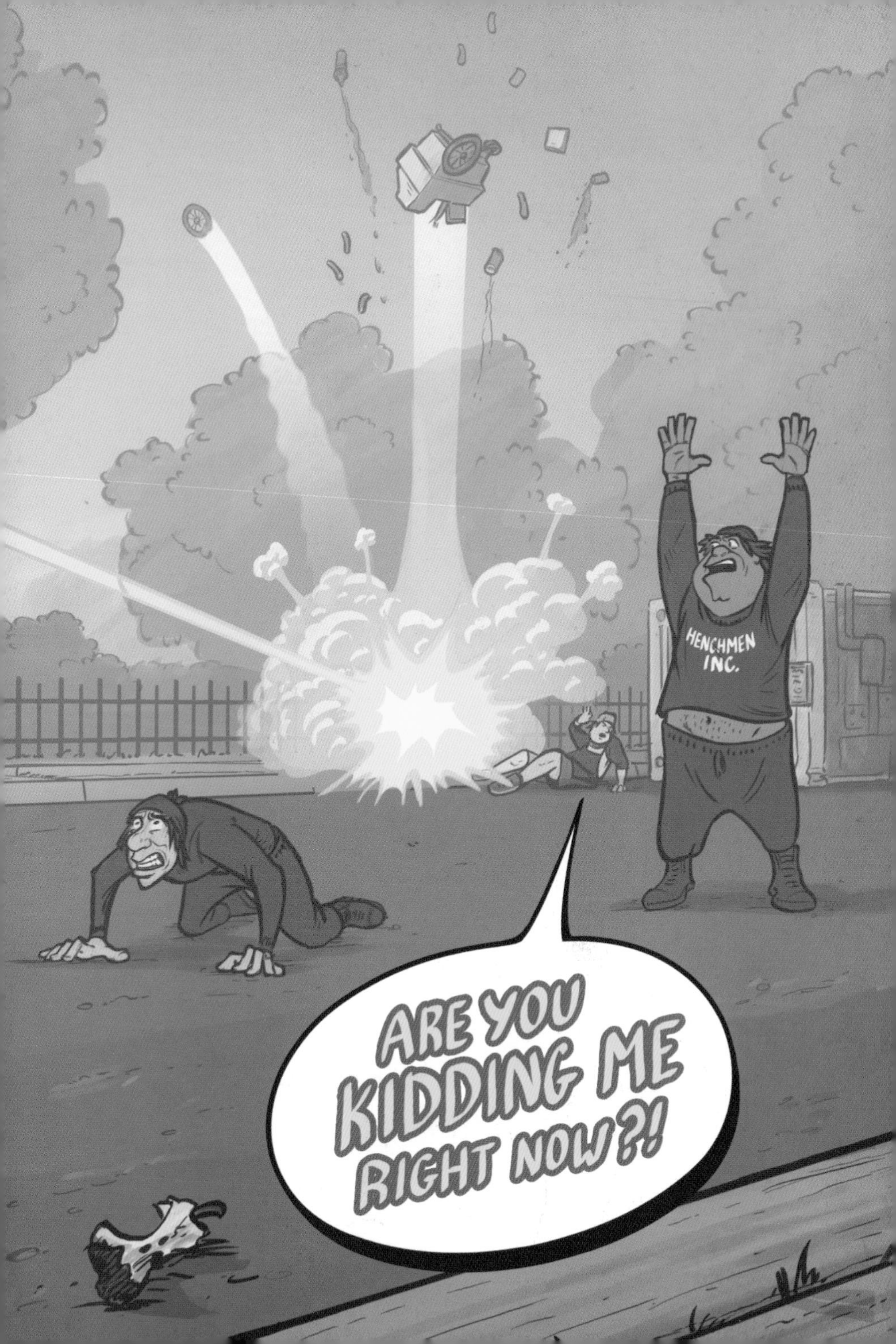
HENCHMEN INC.
ARE YOU KIDDING ME RIGHT NOW?!

Just to rub it in, the jerks in black jumped the fence right next to me.

The cops tried to follow them, but...

Guess who showed up to save the day?

Just to rub it in, the jerks in black jumped the fence right next to me.

The cops tried to follow them, but...

Guess who showed up to save the day?

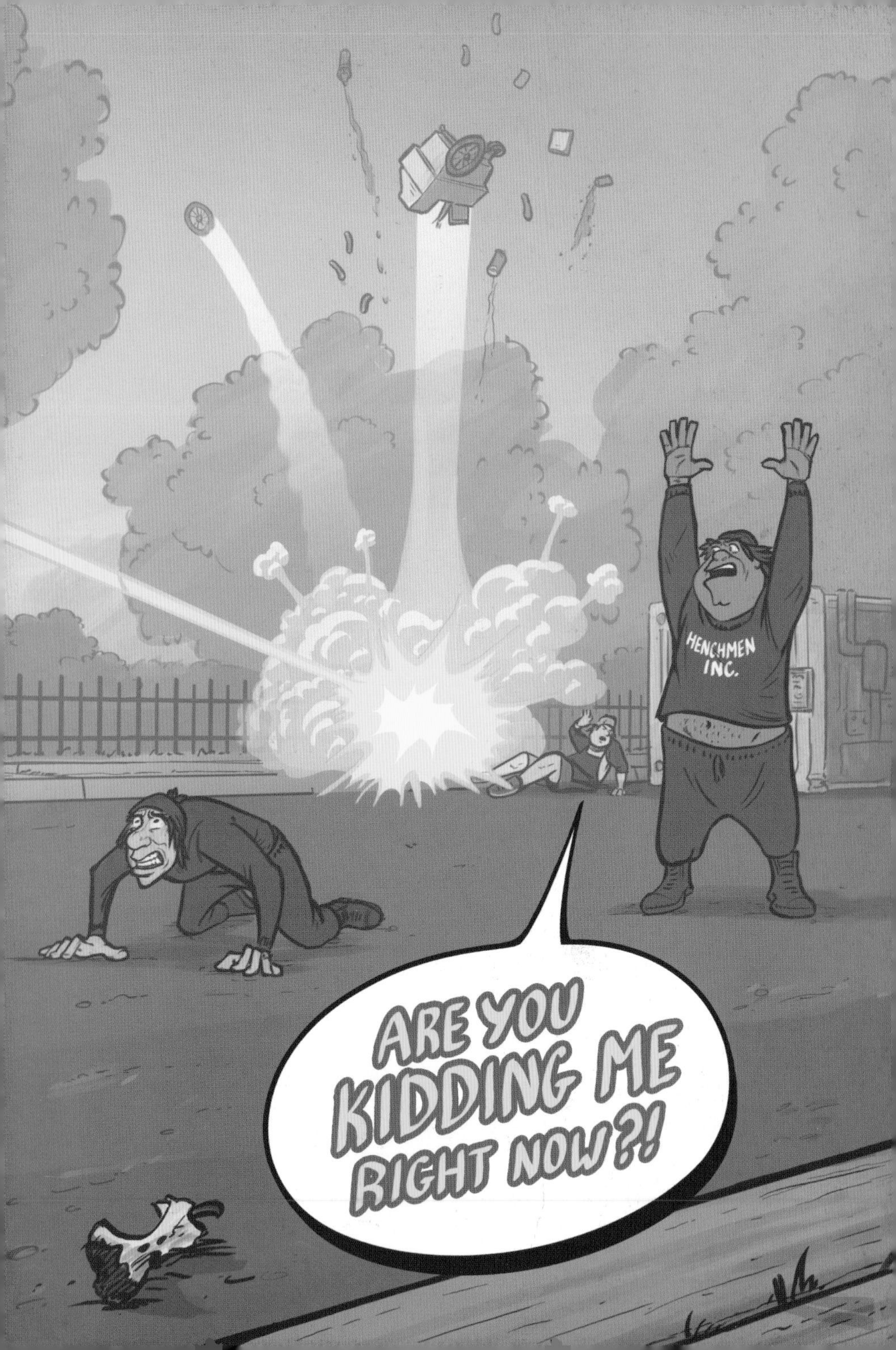
HENCHMEN INC.
ARE YOU KIDDING ME RIGHT NOW?!

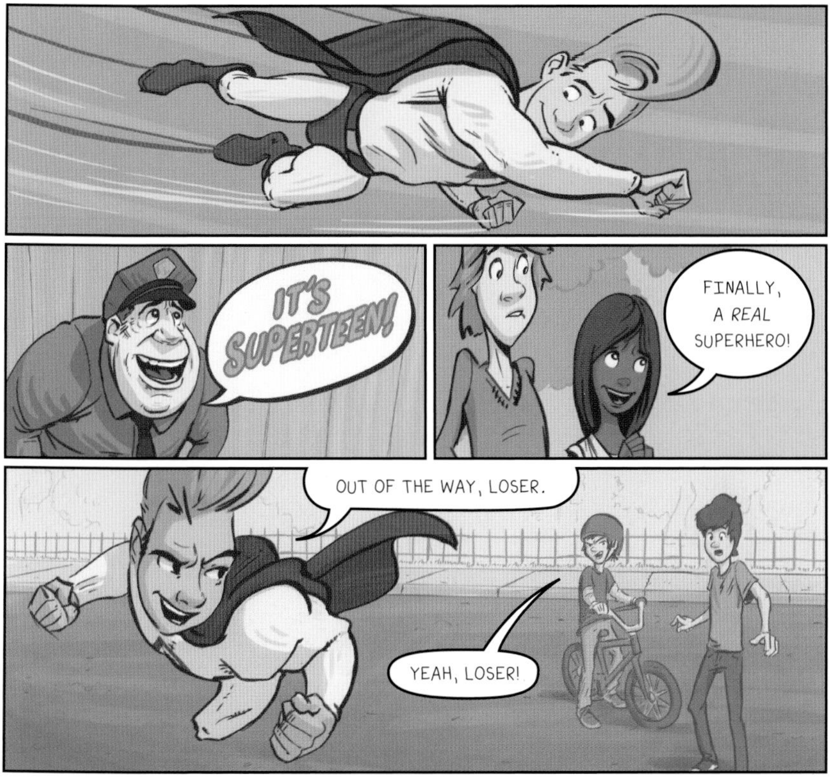
IT'S SUPERTEEN!
FINALLY, A *REAL* SUPERHERO!
OUT OF THE WAY, LOSER.
YEAH, LOSER!

I felt even worse after that.

Trevor rounded up the bad guys in about four seconds, and, of course, everybody cheered.

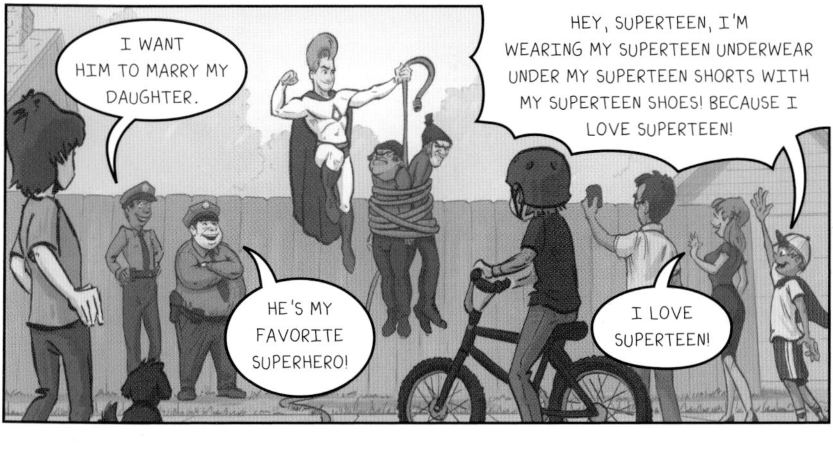
I WANT HIM TO MARRY MY DAUGHTER.
HEY, SUPERTEEN, I'M WEARING MY SUPERTEEN UNDERWEAR UNDER MY SUPERTEEN SHORTS WITH MY SUPERTEEN SHOES! BECAUSE I LOVE SUPERTEEN!
HE'S MY FAVORITE SUPERHERO!
I LOVE SUPERTEEN!

I should have been the one capturing those criminals. And if my stupid lasers had gone straight, I would have. Then everyone would have cheered for *me*.

Once the cops finished taking pictures with Superteen, they put the bad guys in the back of their squad cars.

As if it wasn't bad enough that my lasers blew up a hot dog cart, Trevor had to show up and embarrass me in front of the whole crowd. That was the last time I was going to use my powers. Ever.

Or so I thought.

CHAPTER
THREE

On my way home, I walked by the fence the bad guys had jumped over and noticed a piece of paper on the ground. One of them must have dropped it. I guess everyone had been too busy idolizing Trevor to notice.

There was no way I was going to try and stop whatever was going down at the museum, not after the humiliation I had just gone through.

So when I got home, I called the police to take care of it, but they wouldn't listen to a twelve-year-old with a note from a guy with no name.

So the museum was going to be robbed. I wasn't happy about it, but what could I do? No one would listen to me. Besides, wouldn't it be better to have some thieves steal a few museum pieces than to have my lasers burn the place to the ground?

That afternoon, I sat down to watch some TV and forget about the whole thing, but then a news report came on.

As much as I hated to admit it, Trevor was right. The museum's security guards were in danger. How could I just sit back and let them rob the place when I could at least try to stop them? Like Trevor said, it was my duty—super powers or not.

So it was up to me and Lewis to save the day, which was kind of sad.

Wait, I haven't said anything about Lewis yet, have I? We've been friends for a really long time now, like a whole year. He isn't exactly the most popular kid at school, but then again, neither am I. We hang out because he's the only other kid my age who's still into playing with action figures. Everyone else makes fun of me for it. It's really annoying. Last year, almost everyone I knew played with action figures, and now all of a sudden everyone's too cool for that kind of stuff.

Not Lewis, though. Nothing about Lewis is cool, really, but that's fine by me.

I've got a few more friends at school I hang out with, though. Lewis—not so much. No one really talks to him. At times, I can't say I blame them.

I mean, for one thing, Lewis isn't smart, at all.

LEWIS →

← MY CRAYON

And he almost never says anything unless he's using his powers.

He's a ~~tele teletub~~ . . . uh, Lewis can read other people's minds. The problem is he always reads them out loud.

Which is why my dad hides in the basement when Lewis comes over.

Lewis definitely takes some getting used to.

His mom says he's a little different because he spends so much time in other people's heads.

I'M PRETTY SURE THAT'S *NOT* HIS ONLY PROBLEM.

As you may have guessed, Lewis and I didn't qualify for the Gifted Powers Program at school, so our chances of getting picked up by a superhero team were pretty much zero.

I, for one, seem to make a mess everytime I try to use my powers, even for simple things like using my lasers to cut paper in art class:

ZAPPING TEACHERS PERMANENTLY STAINS YOUR RECORD.

If you think nerds get picked on a lot at school, you should see how Defectives like Lewis and I are treated. That's what people call kids like us with powers that don't work right—Defectives. Beating up a kid with super powers probably makes them feel tough, even if their victim's powers don't work right.

Back to last Friday: I didn't know how much help Lewis would be against real villains, but he was the only help I was going to get. We set up a sleepover at his house for that night so we could sneak out to stop the heist at the museum.

My parents would totally bust us if we ever tried to sneak out of my house, especially after midnight, but Lewis's mom was away at a work conference, and we knew his dad would fall asleep in front of the TV, like always. And nothing wakes him up. I mean, nothing.

We got to work making costumes but couldn't really come up with anything good. When I went through Lewis's old Halloween clothes, the only halfway decent thing I found was an old Zorro outfit.

It was either that or the purple crayon costume he's worn for the last three Halloweens in a row. So, of course, I went with Zorro, which didn't make me happy. I mean, I wanted to look like a superhero but ended up looking like the Hamburglar.

And let's just say that was the last time Lewis would be in charge of designing his own costume.

At midnight, we snuck out the back door and rode our bikes a couple blocks to the museum.

When we got there, everything looked fine until we went around to the back of the building.

This was it! A real crime with real criminals!

The problem? There weren't any real heroes to stop them—just me and a kid with a rubber glove strapped to his skull. We could get seriously hurt ...but we could also get seriously famous if we captured these guys.

If we could stop the bad guys, we'd be heroes, *real* superheroes. We'd get our pictures in the paper, land a bunch of TV interviews, be on lunch boxes—all that cool stuff. Just like the Superteam.

SUPERGUY—SUPERTEAM'S LEADER. HE'S PRETTY MUCH UNSTOPPABLE EXCEPT FOR HIS ONE WEAKNESS: A RARE METAL CALLED ACHILLESIUM.

LED ZAPPLIN—HE CAN CONTROL ALMOST ANYTHING ELECTRONIC.

LYCANINE—HE'S A WEREWOLF THAT CAN TRANSFORM WHENEVER HE WANTS.

HYDRATIA—SHE HAS THE POWER TO TURN HERSELF INTO PURE WATER.

And if Lewis and I pulled this off, we'd be the most popular kids at school. People would want to hang out with us at lunch, and we'd get some sweet selfies with the cheerleaders. Kids might even stop calling me Defective.

Maybe.

CHAPTER
FOUR

Our wildest dreams were about to come true. All we had to do was stop a couple of thugs.

When the coast was clear, Lewis and I snuck in through the back door.

The thieves were loading boxes into the back of a van when an idea hit me: I knew exactly how to stop them.

Lewis was right, which meant I was right, because when Lewis said that, he was reading my mind. What if I missed? Every time I fired my lasers, they ended up hitting the worst possible thing. And in a place like this, the worst possible thing could be a lot of things.

I might get to sit with the cool kids at lunch if I saved the day, but I wouldn't be sitting with anyone if a shark bit me in half!

I could always start my superhero career with something a little less dangerous. I mean, superheroes are always walking old ladies across the street and stuff like that, so I *could* start with something simple and wait for word to get around. Old people always talked about how handsome and polite I was. I could bring a few of them to school so they could talk me up in front of some news reporters or something.

As a rule, I always go with whatever plan has fewer sharks in it, so instead of trying to catch the thieves, Lewis and I headed for the exit. Besides, now that a crime was happening, we could call the cops and probably get our picture in the paper, anyway. That would be a decent start for a superhero.

We were halfway to the door when Lewis had to go and blow our cover.

Lewis just stood there, crying. I'll admit I'm not the best friend in the world, but I wasn't going to leave him there all by himself, surrounded by a bunch of goons.

So I held my breath and fired my lasers.

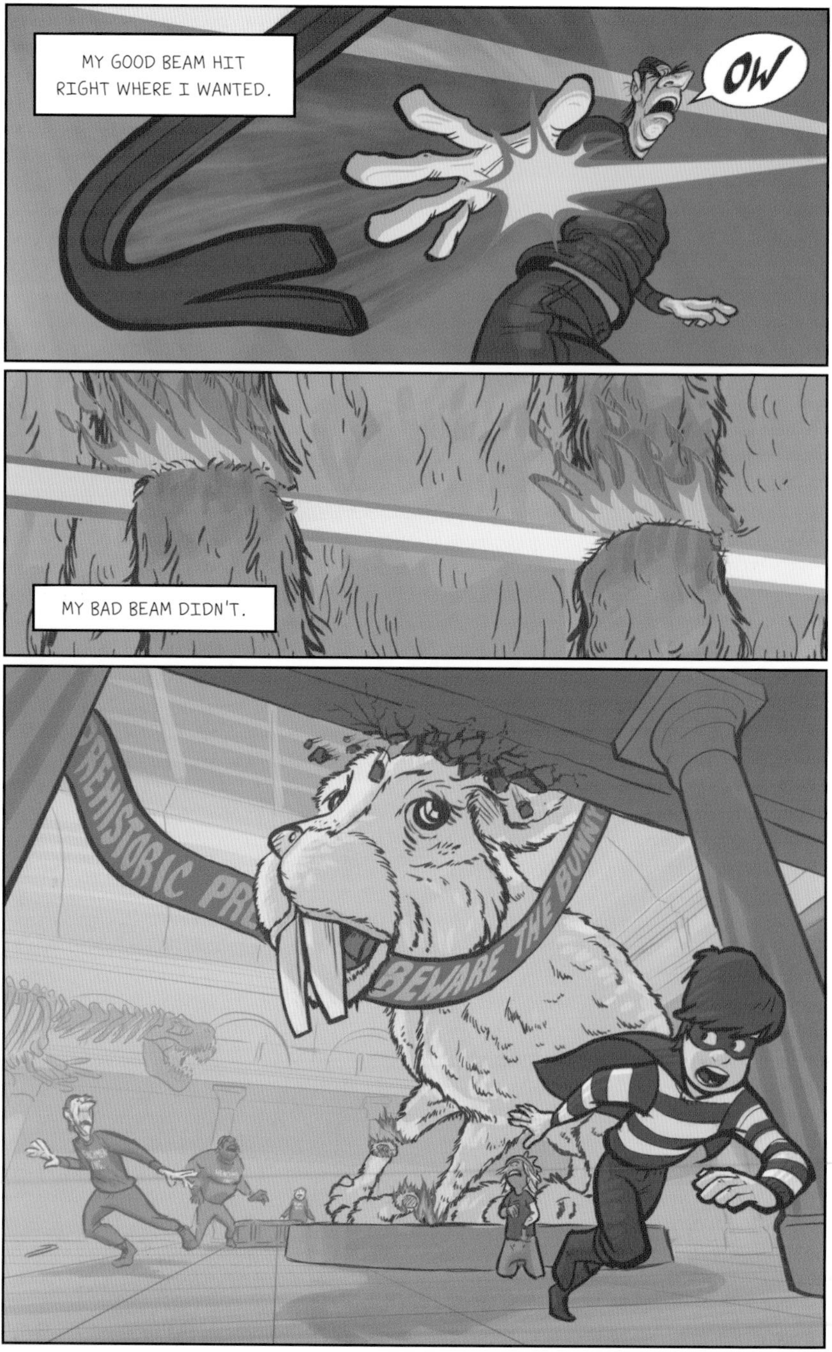
MY GOOD BEAM HIT
RIGHT WHERE I WANTED.
OW
MY BAD BEAM DIDN'T.
PREHISTORIC
BEWARE THE

As if allowing the bad guys to get away wasn't bad enough, I also got a mouth full of fake bunny hair!

At least I hoped it was fake....

Which reminds me, I still need to thank Lewis for all his help.

I THINK THIS ONE'S BROKEN.

You would think, because we were just kids, the robbers would take it easy on us, like call our parents or just kick us out of the museum.

WRONG.

They say your whole life flashes before your eyes when it's about to end, but all I could think was that I didn't want to die dressed like a character from a fast-food restaurant!

The guy was just about to carve me like a pumpkin when ...

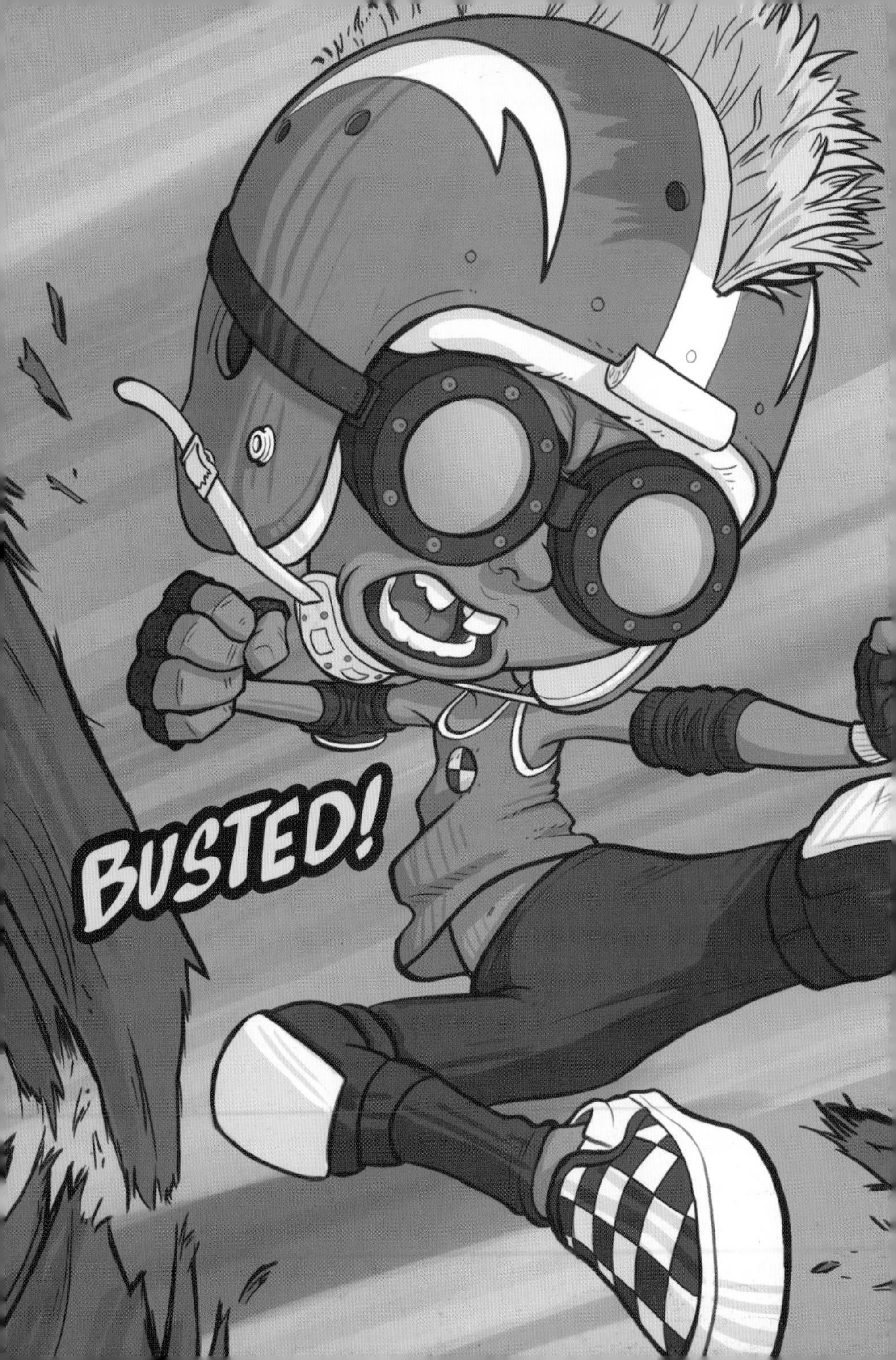
BUSTED!

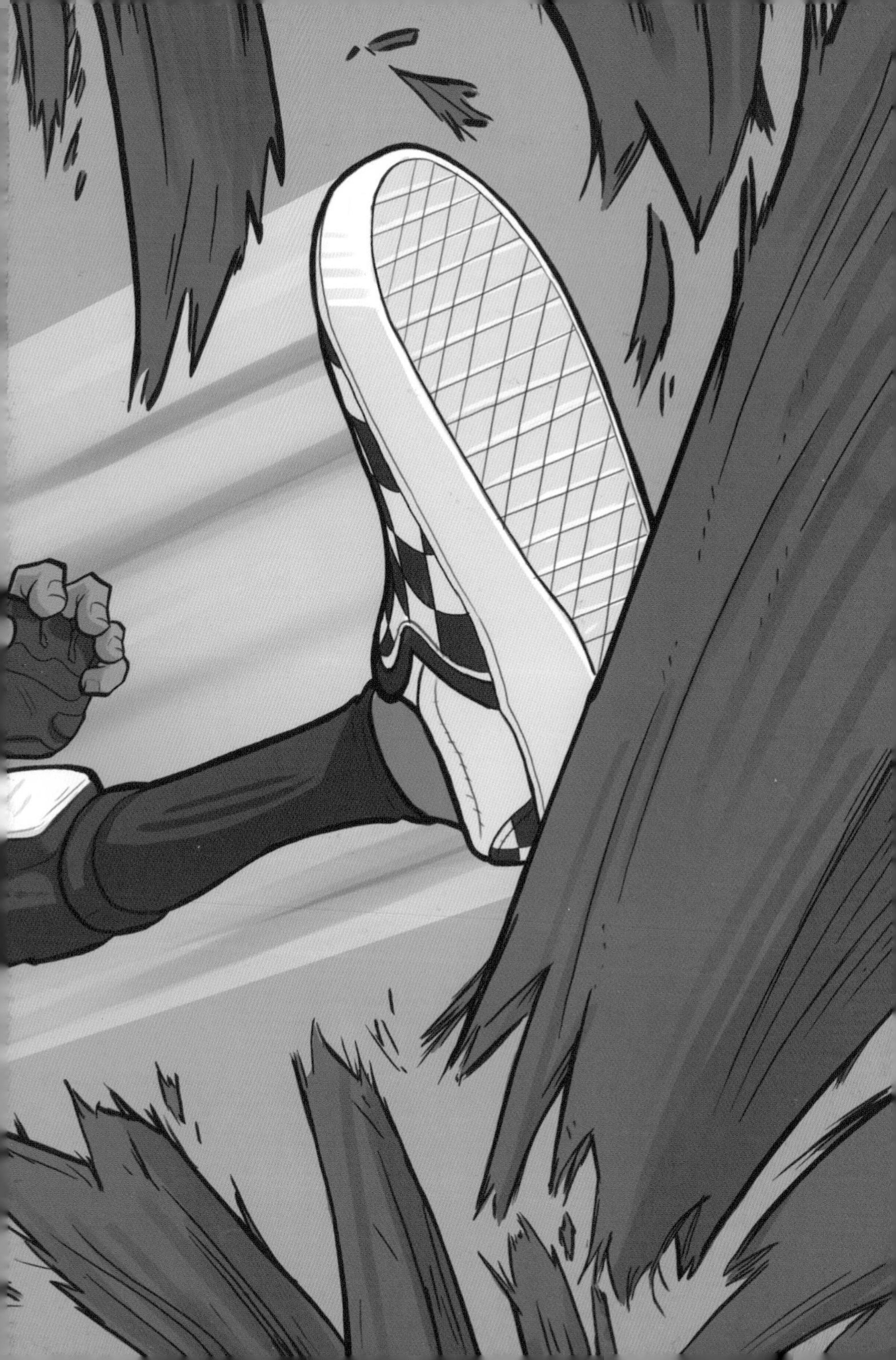

At first, I thought some *real* superheroes had shown up to save us, but it was just Crash and this guy named Tim—two kids who had been kicked out of our school last year. They both have super powers, but they're not much better off than Lewis and me.

Crash can run so fast that he can break the sound barrier! Whatever that is. His only weakness? Stopping.

The same thing happens when he tries to change directions.

HE MEANT TO GO THIS WAY.

Don't get me wrong, I'm glad Crash and Tim showed up, but they weren't exactly the help I was hoping for.

Even though Crash is also pretty much indestructible, his brain gets rattled when he hits stuff too hard.

CLOSE THE GARAGE, MOM. IT'S RAINING.

That's probably why he keeps Tim around.

Because of Tim's powers, you've got to use him as a last resort, which is fine with him. He hates using his powers. When he finally does, boy, you better watch out, no matter what side you're on.

That's when Tim took out his secret weapon: peanuts.

Back when he was still enrolled at our school, Tim would steal other people's lunches all the time. Remember Trevor, the kid who got super powers and stopped the hurricane? Well, the day after the meteor hit Trevor's house, Tim stole the lunch out of Trevor's backpack when he was busy bragging about how great he was.

The problem was that Trevor's mom had made his sandwich the night before and it must have gotten some of the meteor's radiation on it. The meteor gave Trevor some awesome super powers, so Tim might have gotten some pretty sweet powers, too...

So, what happens when you have an allergic reaction to radioactive peanuts?

You grow ten feet tall and smash everything in sight because your throat is swollen shut!

That's when Tim took out his secret weapon: peanuts.

Back when he was still enrolled at our school, Tim would steal other people's lunches all the time. Remember Trevor, the kid who got super powers and stopped the hurricane? Well, the day after the meteor hit Trevor's house, Tim stole the lunch out of Trevor's backpack when he was busy bragging about how great he was.

The problem was that Trevor's mom had made his sandwich the night before and it must have gotten some of the meteor's radiation on it. The meteor gave Trevor some awesome super powers, so Tim might have gotten some pretty sweet powers, too...

So, what happens when you have an allergic reaction to radioactive peanuts?

You grow ten feet tall and smash everything in sight because your throat is swollen shut!

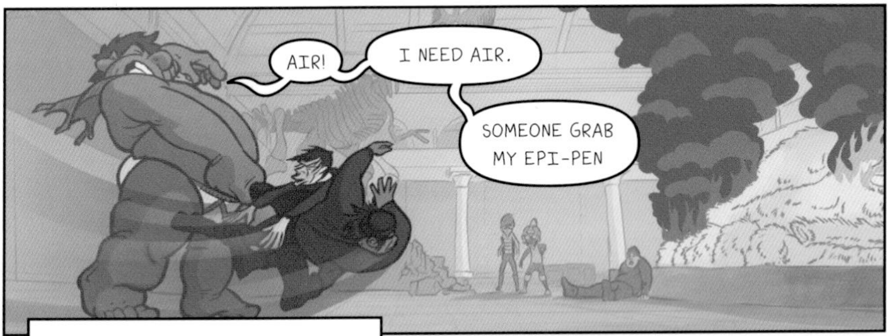
AIR!
I NEED AIR.
SOMEONE GRAB MY EPI-PEN

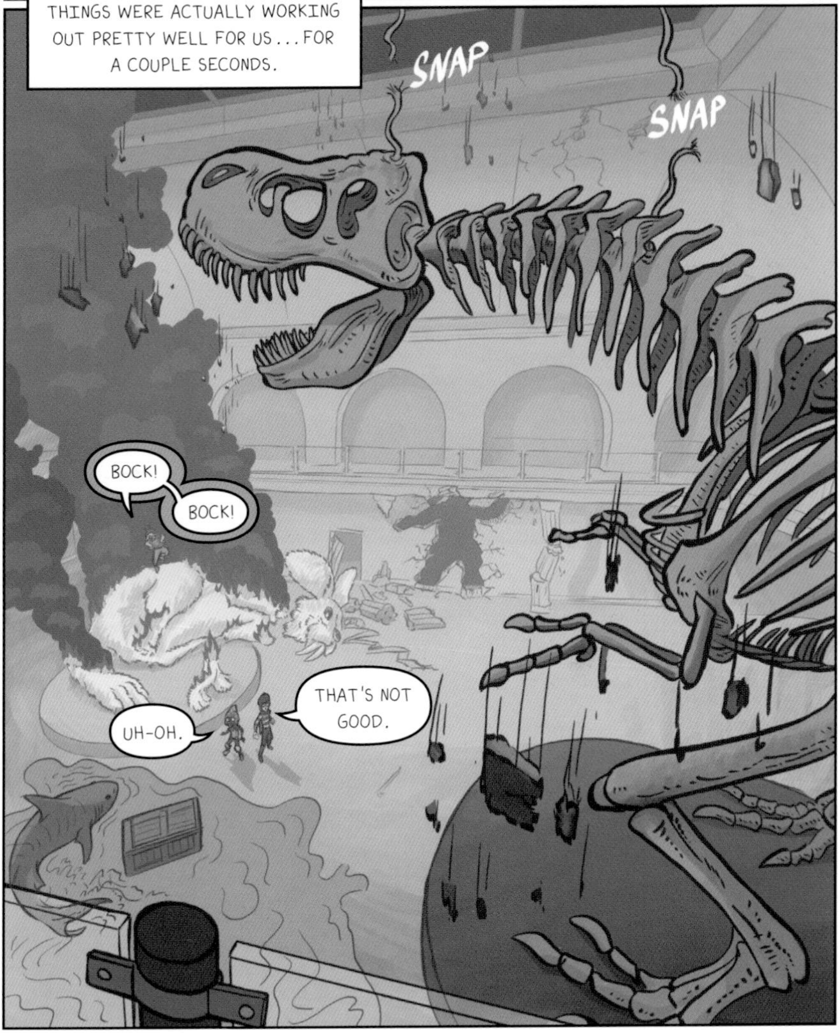
THINGS WERE ACTUALLY WORKING OUT PRETTY WELL FOR US . . . FOR A COUPLE SECONDS.
SNAP
SNAP
BOCK!
BOCK!
UH-OH.
THAT'S NOT GOOD.

The whole building came down right on top of us! Luckily, the dinosaur bones fell first and protected Lewis and me from the falling rubble.

By the time we were able to crawl out, the bad guys had gotten away.

Since I was wearing a costume that made me look just like a burglar, we decided to hightail it out of there before the cops showed up.

After all that, we weren't any closer to becoming superheroes. But on the bright side, we weren't dead.

CHAPTER
FIVE

The next day, I left Lewis's house early. He has a non-slobbered-on version of *Zombiegeddon* that I had planned to play all Saturday, but after what happened at the museum, I really wasn't in the mood. Lewis repeating my thoughts back to me wasn't helping me feel any better, either.

I don't know what I was thinking. Did I really believe I could stop a crime? I mean, I was just a cross-eyed loser with a chicken for a sidekick!

To make things worse, when I got home, Mom told me I had to visit my Uncle Ted with my dad.

I hated going to see Uncle Ted.

It's not that I hate my uncle; I just hated going to *visit* him. He had gone into the hospital two weeks earlier and was on some medication that made him kind of loopy.

I know it wasn't his fault, but it made things pretty awkward. Maybe I should have just done what my dad did—play along with his crazy antics.

You might think my dad is a pretty horrible person for teasing someone on medication, but when he was growing up, my Uncle Ted picked on my dad a lot. He would break my dad's stuff, punch him just for the fun of it, and give him wedgies in front of his friends. You would think now that they're older, all that would be water under the bridge, but Uncle Ted never really grew out of it.

I think teasing Uncle Ted in the hospital was my dad's way of getting back at him.

My Uncle Ted had taken his medications just before we arrived at the hospital, so he was out cold by the time we made it up to his room. The nurse said he would be asleep for a few hours. My dad tried to wake him up anyway, and the nurse got so mad, I thought my dad was going to get a needle in the eye! As for me, I was just happy I was saved from a couple hours of very uncomfortable conversation.

On our way out, Dad used the bathroom and was in there for a really long time. When he finally walked back into the lobby, he was ticked. He told me the stall he was in didn't have any toilet paper, and by the time he realized it, it was too late.

I have no idea how he ended up getting some, but it must have been difficult, because when he came out, he was out of breath and his sleeves were wet up to his shoulders.

Anyway, he complained to the person at the front desk about the lack of extra rolls in the stalls, but apparently Dad didn't like the attitude she gave him. He demanded to speak with her supervisor.

I wasn't allowed to bring my Nintendo DS into the hospital with me, so I was basically dying of boredom while we waited for my dad to complain to the right person. I was halfway through counting the ceiling tiles when this old guy snuck up on me and almost made me pee my pants!

I don't know if you've ever had someone come up behind you when you weren't expecting, and then start hooting like an owl, but it's terrifying. And weird. Really, really weird.

The hooting was strange enough, but it was what the nut job said next that truly freaked me out.

SO, THINGS DIDN'T GO QUITE LIKE YOU PLANNED AT THE MUSEUM LAST NIGHT, DID THEY? WHAT'S YOUR SUPER POWER ANYWAY?

WHO, ME? SUPER POWER? NO. THAT'S CRAZY. YOU'RE CRAZY.... STOP STARING AT ME.

I'm not the best liar, but even if I had been, the old man had undeniable proof I was involved with the museum's destruction. And it was all because I didn't shower like my mom had asked me to.

The guy was good.

He told me his name was The Night Owl and that he used to be a crime fighter when he was younger.

He had been following a recent string of crimes, and the museum heist was the third robbery by the same group of bad guys. I pulled the note from The Man With No Name out of my pocket. When I showed it to him, he jumped around and did that hooting thing again . . .

The old guy told me that The Man With No Name was his archenemy. Apparently, The Night Owl and his former sidekick, Bluejay, had hunted The Man With No Name for years, but the villain had always managed to escape.

Apparently, many years ago, The Man With No Name had threatened to blow up an entire city if his ransom wasn't paid. The Night Owl followed clues left behind by his nemesis, and when he discovered the location of the bomb, he made sure the city was evacuated before anyone could get hurt.

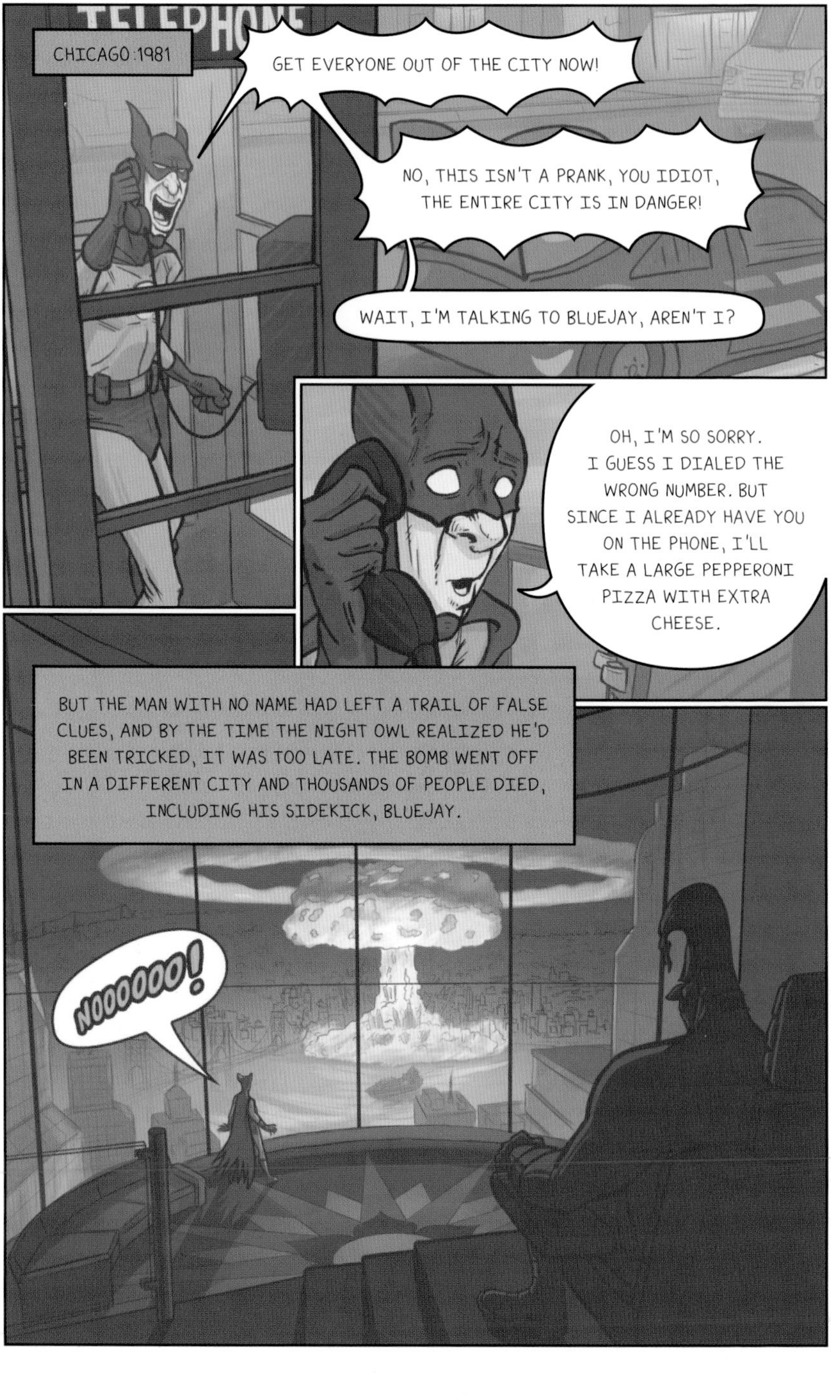
TELEPHONE
CHICAGO 1981
GET EVERYONE OUT OF THE CITY NOW!
NO, THIS ISN'T A PRANK, YOU IDIOT, THE ENTIRE CITY IS IN DANGER!
WAIT, I'M TALKING TO BLUEJAY, AREN'T I?
OH, I'M SO SORRY. I GUESS I DIALED THE WRONG NUMBER. BUT SINCE I ALREADY HAVE YOU ON THE PHONE, I'LL TAKE A LARGE PEPPERONI PIZZA WITH EXTRA CHEESE.
BUT THE MAN WITH NO NAME HAD LEFT A TRAIL OF FALSE CLUES, AND BY THE TIME THE NIGHT OWL REALIZED HE'D BEEN TRICKED, IT WAS TOO LATE. THE BOMB WENT OFF IN A DIFFERENT CITY AND THOUSANDS OF PEOPLE DIED, INCLUDING HIS SIDEKICK, BLUEJAY.
NOOOOOO!

A year or two later, he threatened to blow up a city again, but this time The Man With No Name's ransom was paid immediately. Then he disappeared without a trace.

Everyone blamed The Night Owl for what happened to the city—and to Bluejay. For years, he hunted The Man With No Name, but the villain never resurfaced.

I told him I was sorry he had lost his sidekick, but nothing he could say was going to talk me into helping him. Then the old geezer threatened to tell the cops I was one of the kids who turned the museum into a smoking pile of rubble.

So, it was either help an old man chase a supervillain until his afternoon nap or go to jail. It was kind of a no-brainer.

The Night Owl got so worked up when I told him about what happened at the museum that some of the hospital workers ran over to calm him down, but he threw some kind of smoke bomb and disappeared....

By the way, if you're ever bored, I recommend you pay a visit to the hospital where my Uncle Ted is staying and throw a smoke bomb, because when The Night Owl did it, everyone went nuts. It was awesome.

The smoke bomb also gave me a chance to get out of there before the old man could turn me in, so I ran to my dad and pretended I had to use the bathroom.

The first thing I did when I got home was throw away the seashell stuck to my shoe and beeline it to the bathroom. I didn't want the cops to catch on to the clues The Night Owl had found, trace them back to me, and throw me in jail, so I decided to take a shower and get rid of all signs that I had ever been at the museum.

I was feeling pretty down, though. It was bad enough that Lewis and I had destroyed the museum and the bad guys had gotten away...

CRASH
July 24, 9:30 am

Really blew it at the museum last night!
#embarrassing #sadface #itwastimsfault
@MarshallHerbertPreston @LewisIsAwesome @PBTim_monster.

51.2 Views
MUSEUM HEIST
XYZ NEWS.COM/129834765/htm
👍 Like   💬 Comment   ➤ Share

I made Crash take down the status so, you know, *we wouldn't be arrested.* But it had already been up for five minutes so I knew everyone at school had probably already seen it.

That one post would be enough to cripple my social life forever.

The only way to save myself from an entire school year of wedgies and spit wads was to find and catch the bad guys from the museum.

Too bad I had absolutely no way of doing either of those things.

The way I saw it, I had only one way out of this mess: I had to fake my own death and move far, far away.

I was debating whether my new name should be Jimmy McSly or Zak Rad when I got a phone call.

It was The Night Owl.

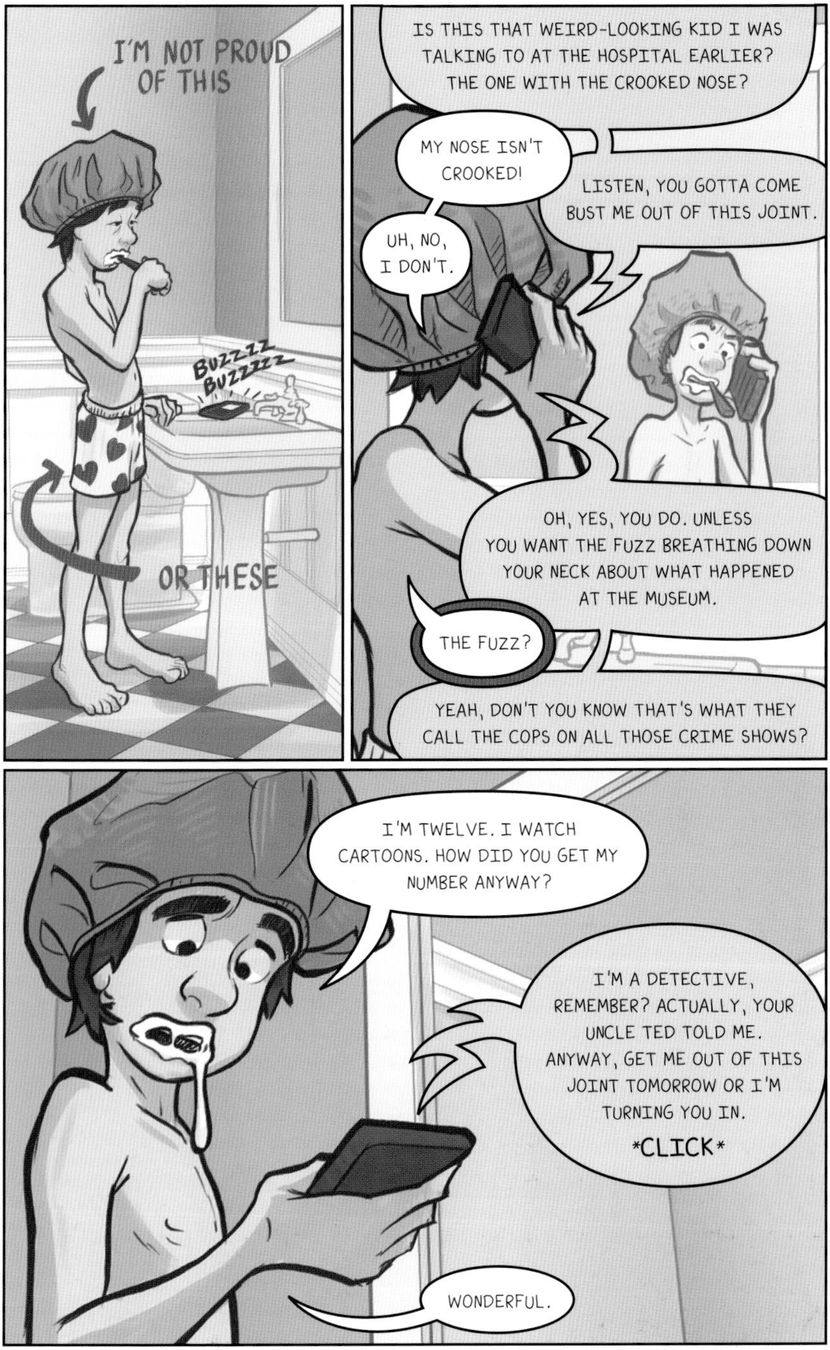
I'M NOT PROUD OF THIS
BUZZZZ BUZZZZZ
OR THESE
IS THIS THAT WEIRD-LOOKING KID I WAS TALKING TO AT THE HOSPITAL EARLIER? THE ONE WITH THE CROOKED NOSE?
MY NOSE ISN'T CROOKED!
LISTEN, YOU GOTTA COME BUST ME OUT OF THIS JOINT.
UH, NO, I DON'T.
OH, YES, YOU DO. UNLESS YOU WANT THE FUZZ BREATHING DOWN YOUR NECK ABOUT WHAT HAPPENED AT THE MUSEUM.
THE FUZZ?
YEAH, DON'T YOU KNOW THAT'S WHAT THEY CALL THE COPS ON ALL THOSE CRIME SHOWS?
I'M TWELVE. I WATCH CARTOONS. HOW DID YOU GET MY NUMBER ANYWAY?
I'M A DETECTIVE, REMEMBER? ACTUALLY, YOUR UNCLE TED TOLD ME. ANYWAY, GET ME OUT OF THIS JOINT TOMORROW OR I'M TURNING YOU IN.
CLICK
WONDERFUL.

CHAPTER
SIX

On Monday morning, I told my mom I wanted to visit Uncle Ted again. She almost had a heart attack.

I called up Lewis and we rode our bikes to the hospital.

The Night Owl sure was excited to see us. I don't think he got many visitors.

I introduced him to Lewis, who, of course, responded the way only he could.

Okay, that time Lewis was reading *my* thoughts. Of course, I wasn't going to admit to it, but it needed to be said. Our football team's armpits smelled better than The Night Owl's breath. And I'm speaking from experience.

The Night Owl told us he was scheduled to have an operation to get his bunions removed, so there was no way the hospital was going to let him leave. We were going to have to break him out. He handed me and Lewis a few things that looked like owl lawn ornaments. I asked him what the heck they were, and he said, "You'll see." Then he told us to go to his car, open it, and wait for him in the parking lot.

It wasn't tough to figure out which car was his.

I really didn't want to help some crazy old guy escape from a hospital, but the last thing I needed was to end up in jail for wrecking the museum, so I didn't have much of a choice. Besides, The Night Owl actually seemed like he was a decent detective, and maybe he'd be able to help me clear my name and catch the bad guys after all.

Lewis and I didn't have to wait long before we heard an explosion in the hospital lobby and The Night Owl sprinted out the front doors.

We threw the lawn ornaments on the ground, and they sprayed this weird goo all over the sidewalk.

The three of us jumped into the car and burned rubber out of there.

When we pulled up to what was left of the museum, the cops stopped us.

The Night Owl stormed off and climbed a tree.

We finally got the old man up the tree, and he took out some binoculars. He looked through them for a few seconds, and then wanted us to get him down. If you thought getting him into the tree was tough, you should have seen us getting him out!

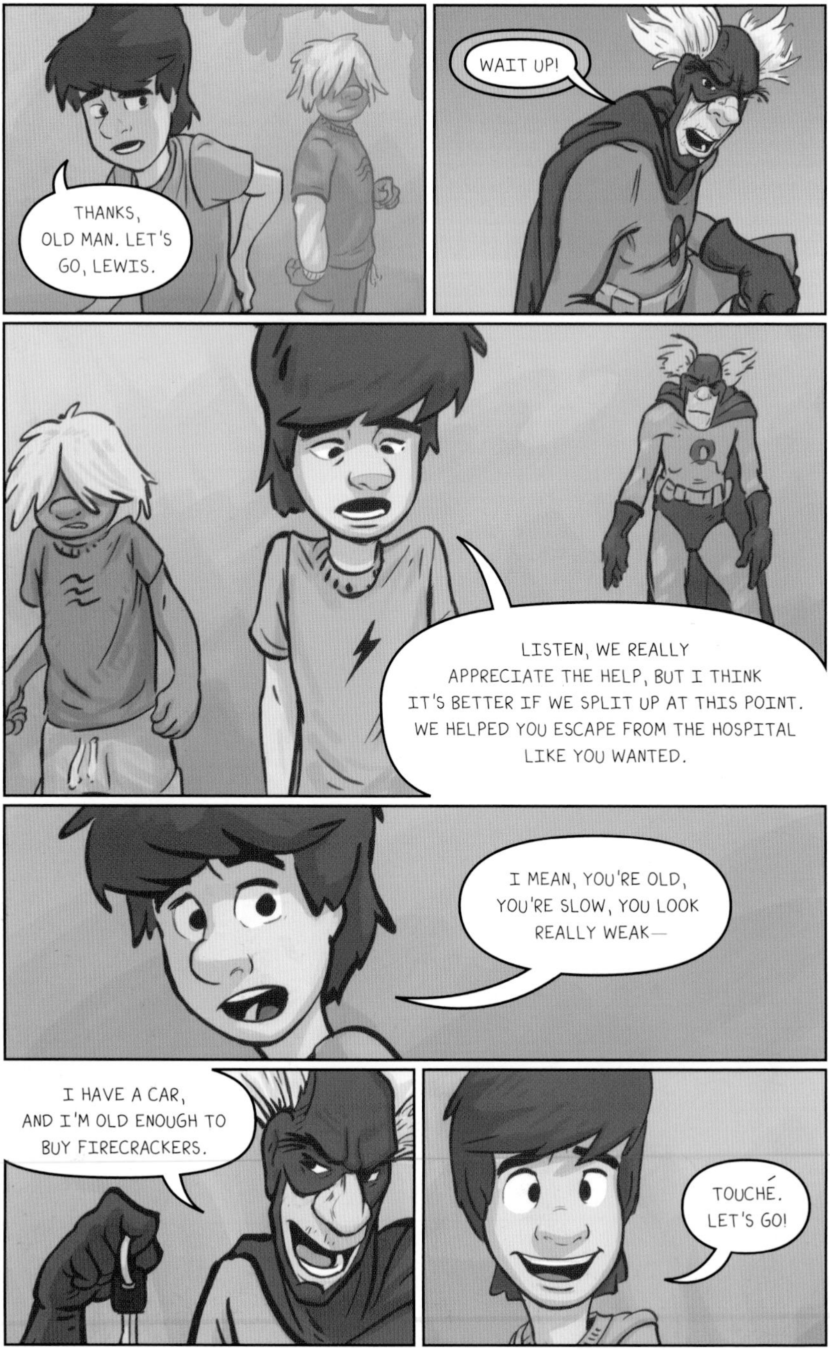
THANKS, OLD MAN. LET'S GO, LEWIS.
WAIT UP!
LISTEN, WE REALLY APPRECIATE THE HELP, BUT I THINK IT'S BETTER IF WE SPLIT UP AT THIS POINT. WE HELPED YOU ESCAPE FROM THE HOSPITAL LIKE YOU WANTED.
I MEAN, YOU'RE OLD, YOU'RE SLOW, YOU LOOK REALLY WEAK—
I HAVE A CAR, AND I'M OLD ENOUGH TO BUY FIRECRACKERS.
TOUCHÉ. LET'S GO!

Lewis and I leaped into the car. The Night Owl took a bit longer.

When we finally got to the construction site, the workers stopped us at the front gate.

But we weren't about to give up. We drove up a hill behind the site to get a better look. Turns out, it wasn't just any old construction site.

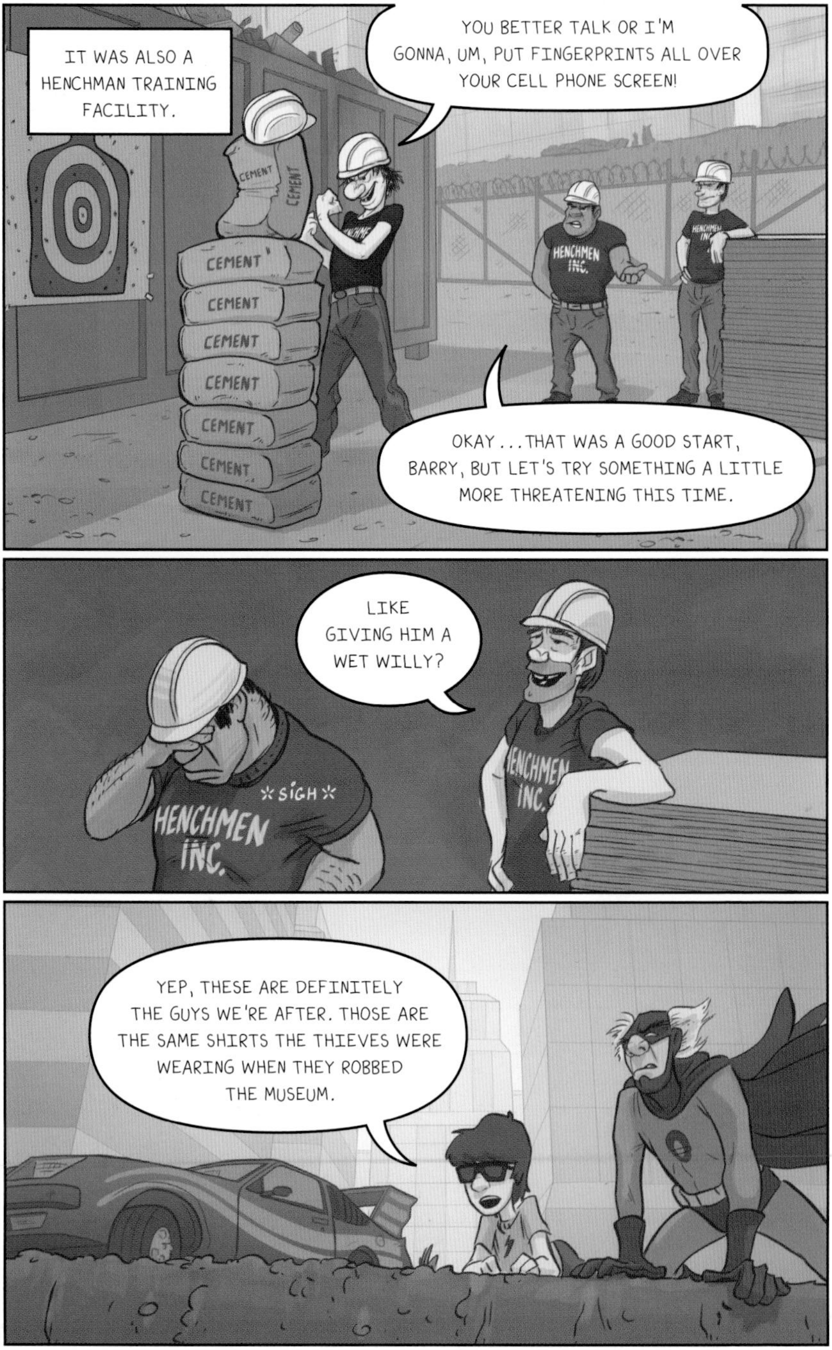
IT WAS ALSO A HENCHMAN TRAINING FACILITY.
YOU BETTER TALK OR I'M GONNA, UM, PUT FINGERPRINTS ALL OVER YOUR CELL PHONE SCREEN!
CEMENT
HENCHMEN INC.
OKAY . . . THAT WAS A GOOD START, BARRY, BUT LET'S TRY SOMETHING A LITTLE MORE THREATENING THIS TIME.
LIKE GIVING HIM A WET WILLY?
SIGH
HENCHMEN INC.
YEP, THESE ARE DEFINITELY THE GUYS WE'RE AFTER. THOSE ARE THE SAME SHIRTS THE THIEVES WERE WEARING WHEN THEY ROBBED THE MUSEUM.

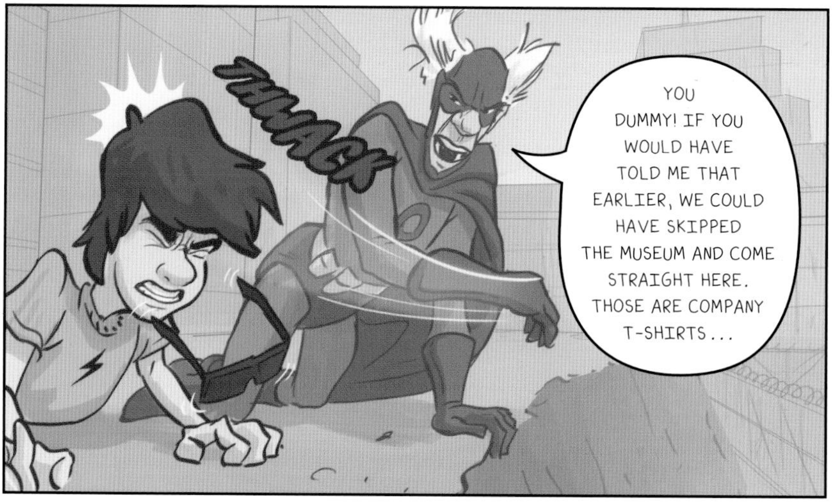
THWACK
YOU DUMMY! IF YOU WOULD HAVE TOLD ME THAT EARLIER, WE COULD HAVE SKIPPED THE MUSEUM AND COME STRAIGHT HERE. THOSE ARE COMPANY T-SHIRTS . . .

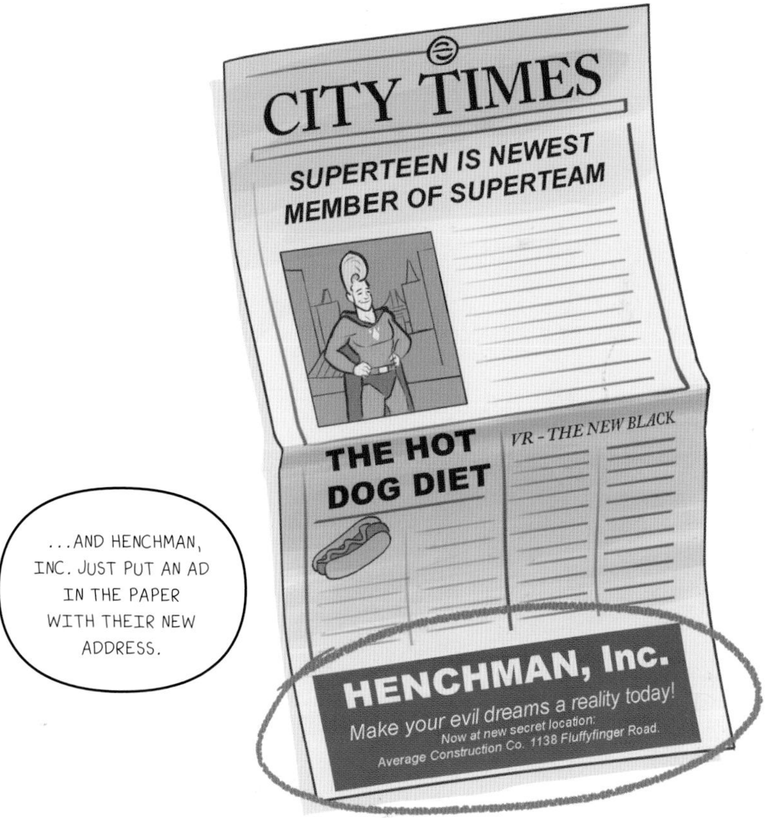
. . .AND HENCHMAN, INC. JUST PUT AN AD IN THE PAPER WITH THEIR NEW ADDRESS.
CITY TIMES
SUPERTEEN IS NEWEST MEMBER OF SUPERTEAM
THE HOT DOG DIET
VR - THE NEW BLACK
HENCHMAN, Inc.
Make your evil dreams a reality today!
Now at new secret location:
Average Construction Co. 1138 Fluffyfinger Road.

CHAPTER
SEVEN

We slid down the hill, climbed under the fence, and hid behind a stack of barrels. One of the guards got a little too close, but The Night Owl was ready for him. Sort of.

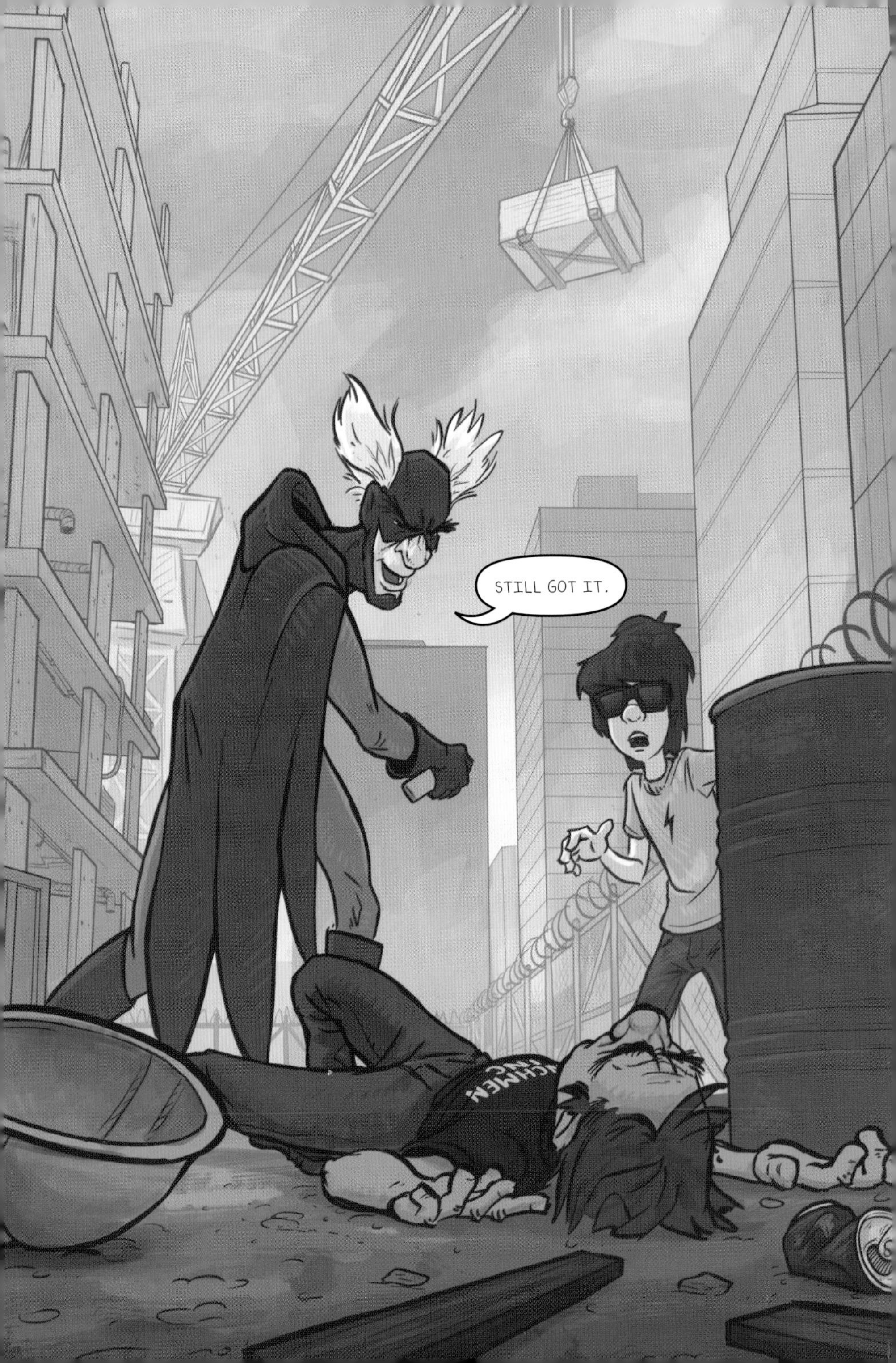
STILL GOT IT.

We snuck around to the trailers in back of the main construction area.

My lasers cut right through the lock . . .

Luckily, only one guy was inside, and we got the drop on him.

The other guys outside had finally noticed the trailer had been sliced in half, so we had to get out of there fast.

I still wasn't sure how we were going to catch The Man With No Name, but The Night Owl didn't seem too worried. I guess his archenemy liked to do things the old-fashioned way.

To me, the old-fashioned way would mean mailing a check, but apparently he meant the *really* old-fashioned way.

The Night Owl just smiled.

CHAPTER EIGHT

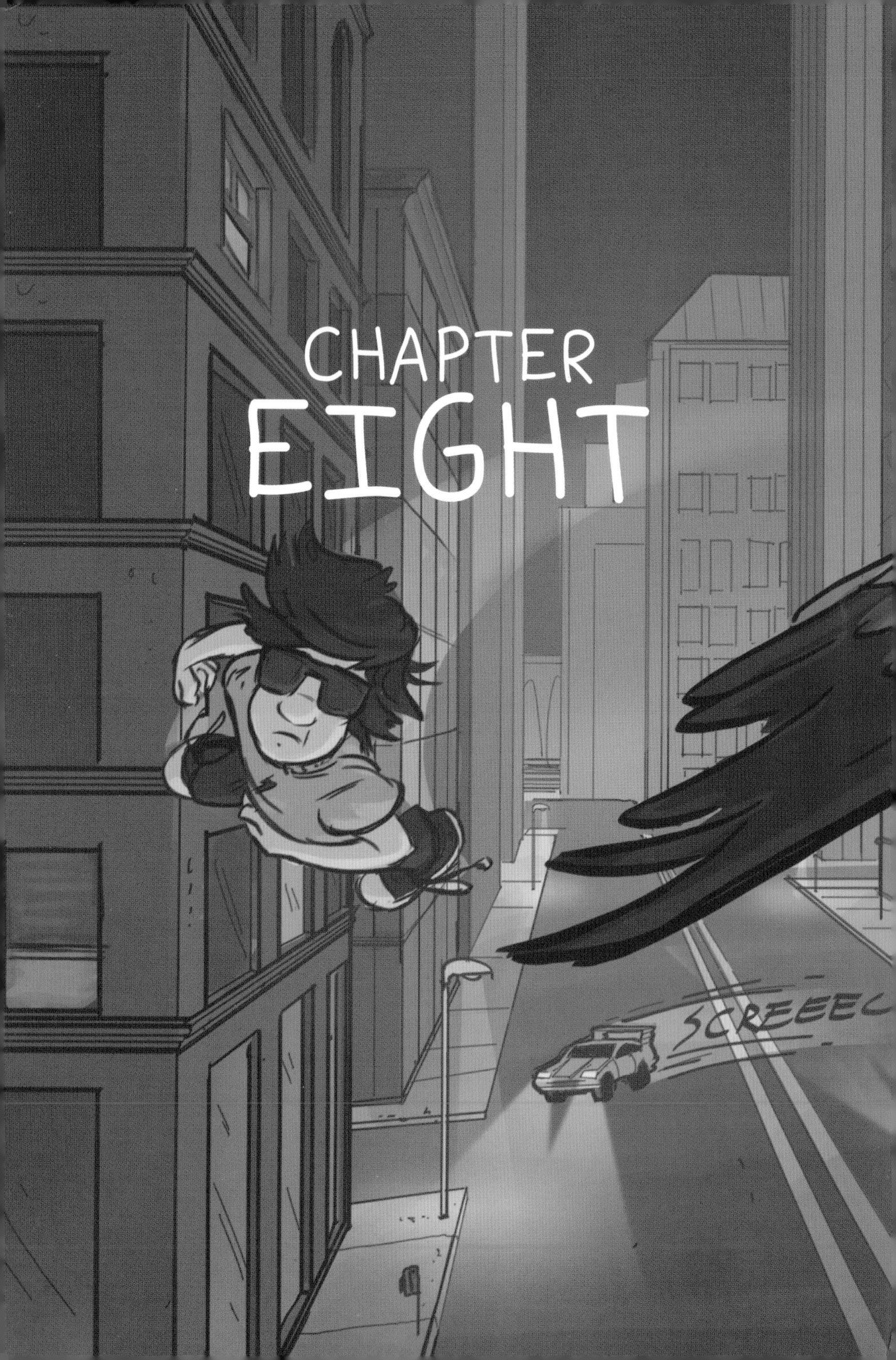
SCREEEC

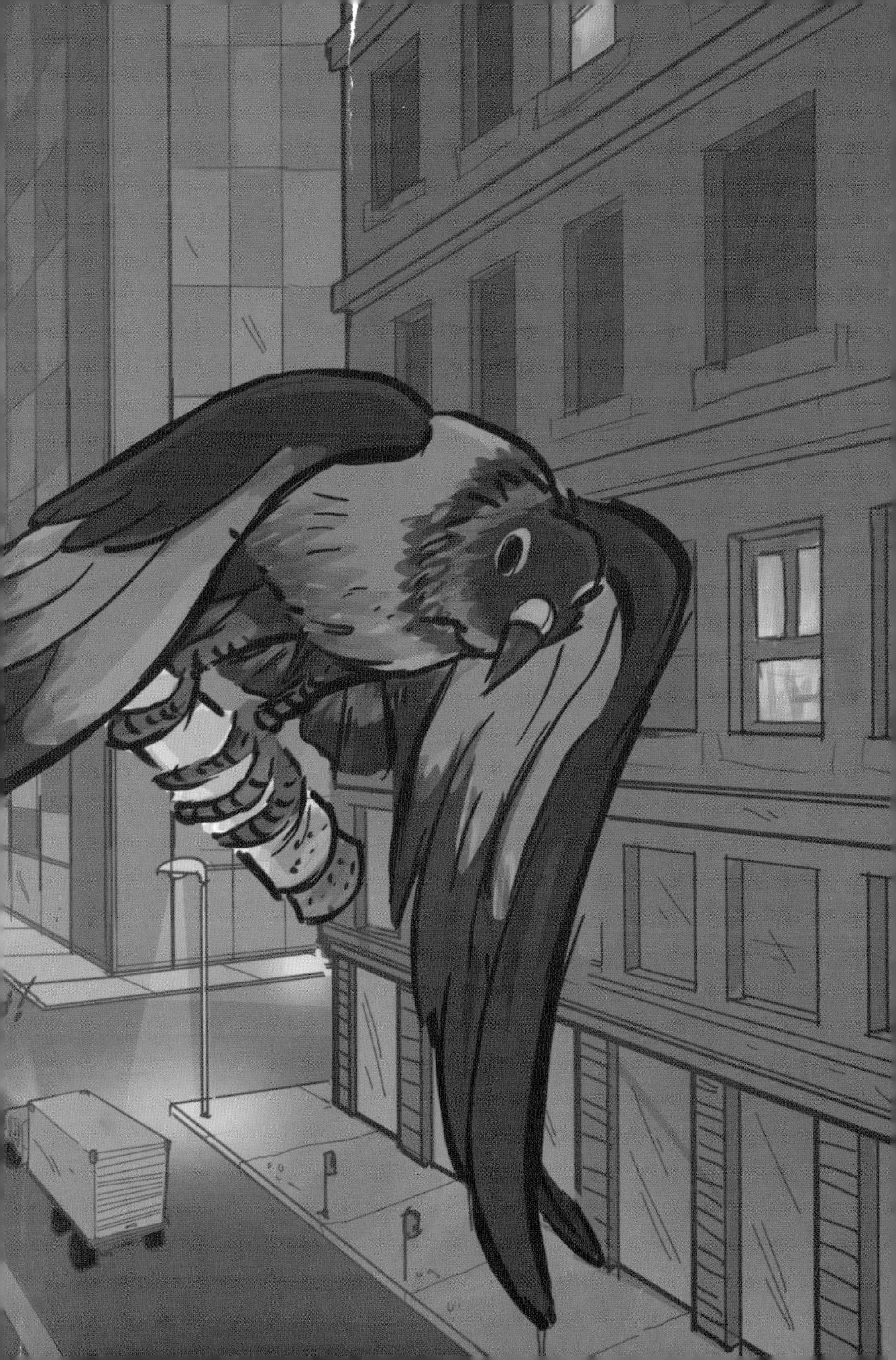

There I was, trying not to puke my brains out while I chased this stupid
pigeon all around town.

He was right.

The pigeon *finally* landed. I hadn't flown for that long in my entire life, and I decided I was *never* going to fly again as long as I lived.

I HOPE THEIR ROOF DOESN'T LEAK!

I finished barfing my brains out and peeked over the edge of the roof. When I saw who was there to pick up the pigeon, I almost fell off the building.

IT WAS NONE OTHER THAN DEBBIE PINSO.

I had history class with her last year. Debbie has the power to control animals, which is actually a sweet power.

But because we live in the city, the only animals for her to control are the kind you don't even want near you, like opossums, pigeons, and cockroaches.

She hadn't made it into the Gifted Powers Program, either.

I had no idea why Debbie would be the one picking up the pigeon sent by The Man With No Name.

That was when The Night Owl and Lewis showed up.

They jumped out of the car and tried to catch her, but Debbie took off. We chased after her for about a block, finally cornering her at the end of an alley.

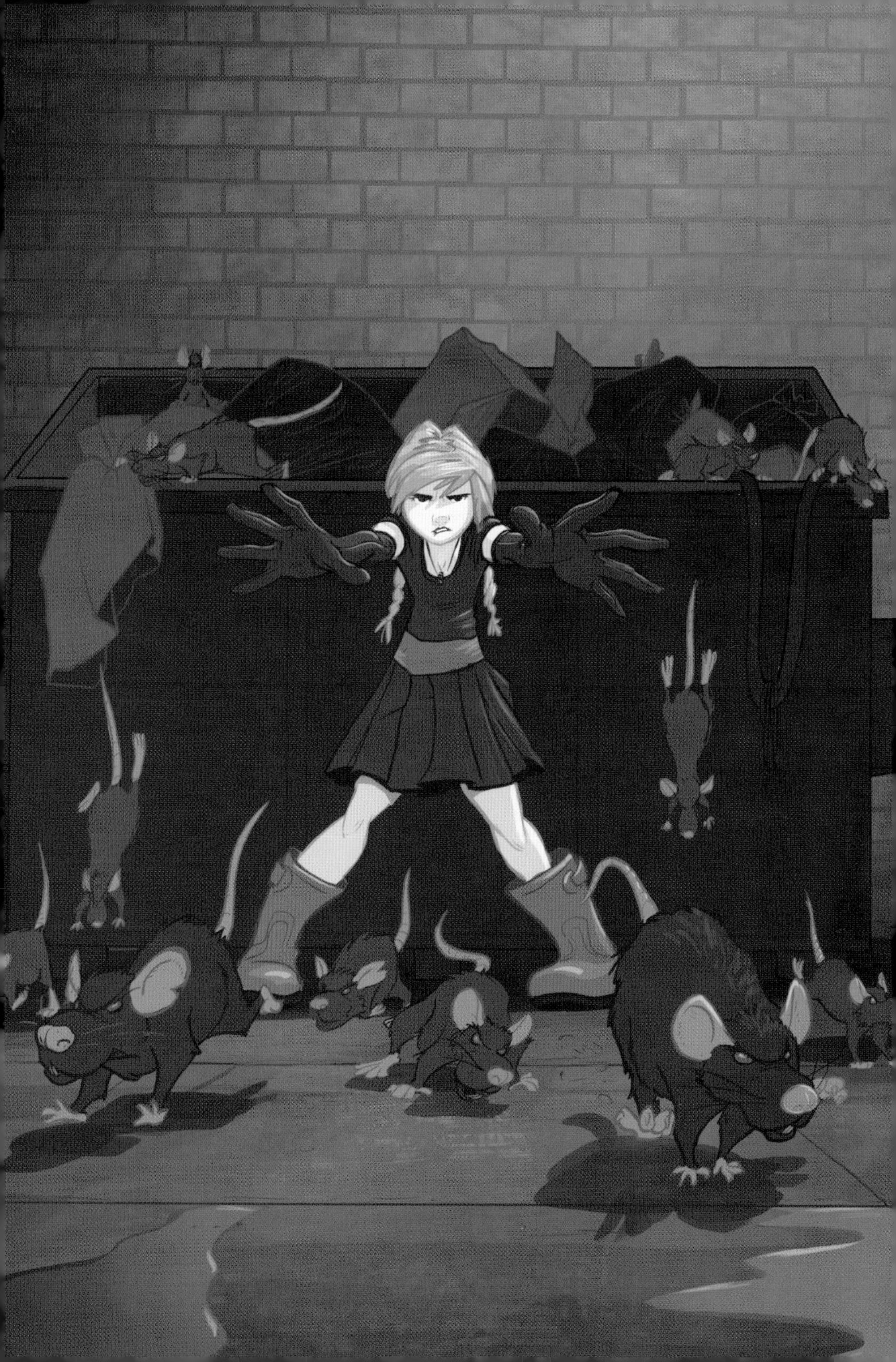

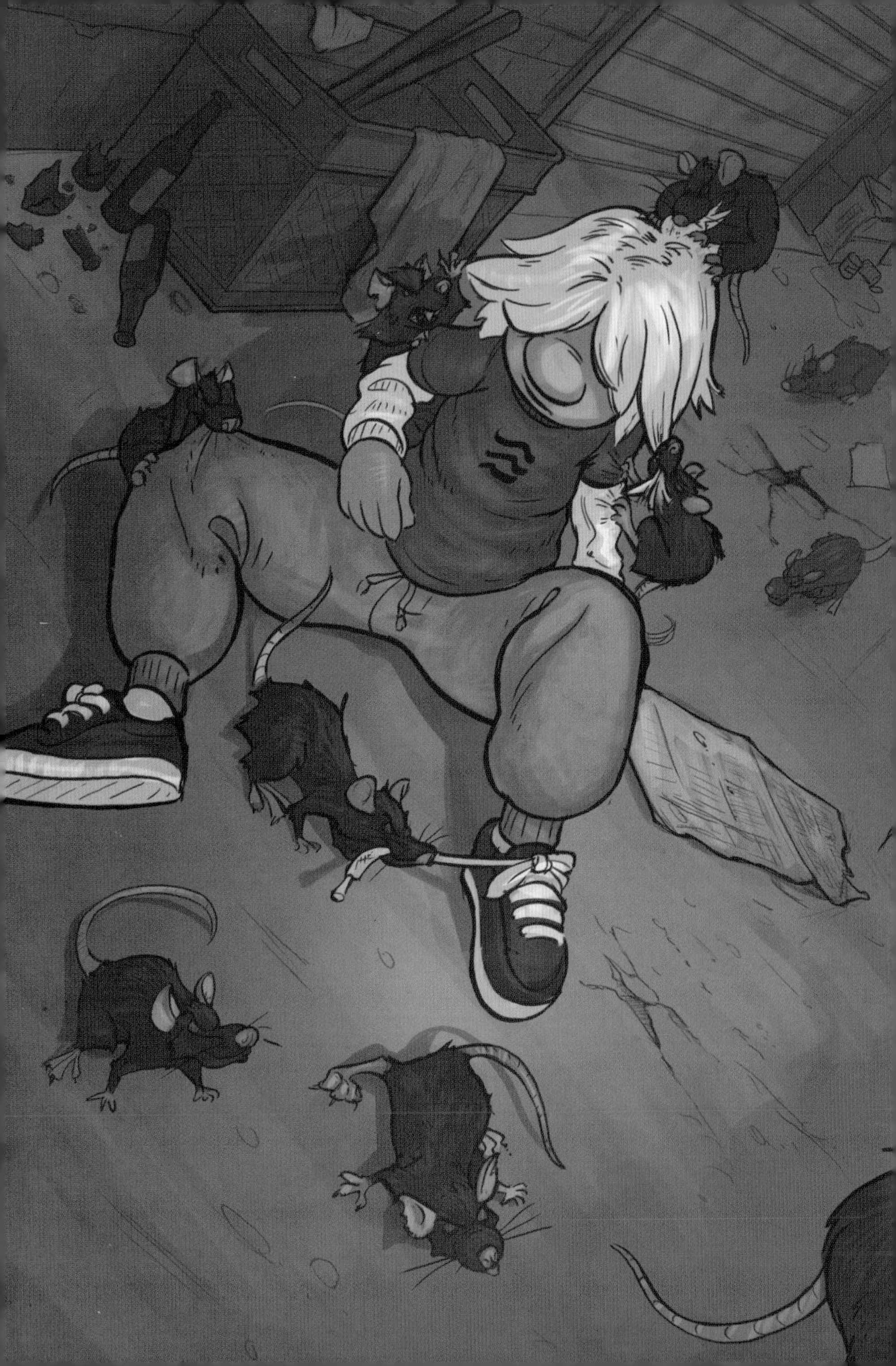

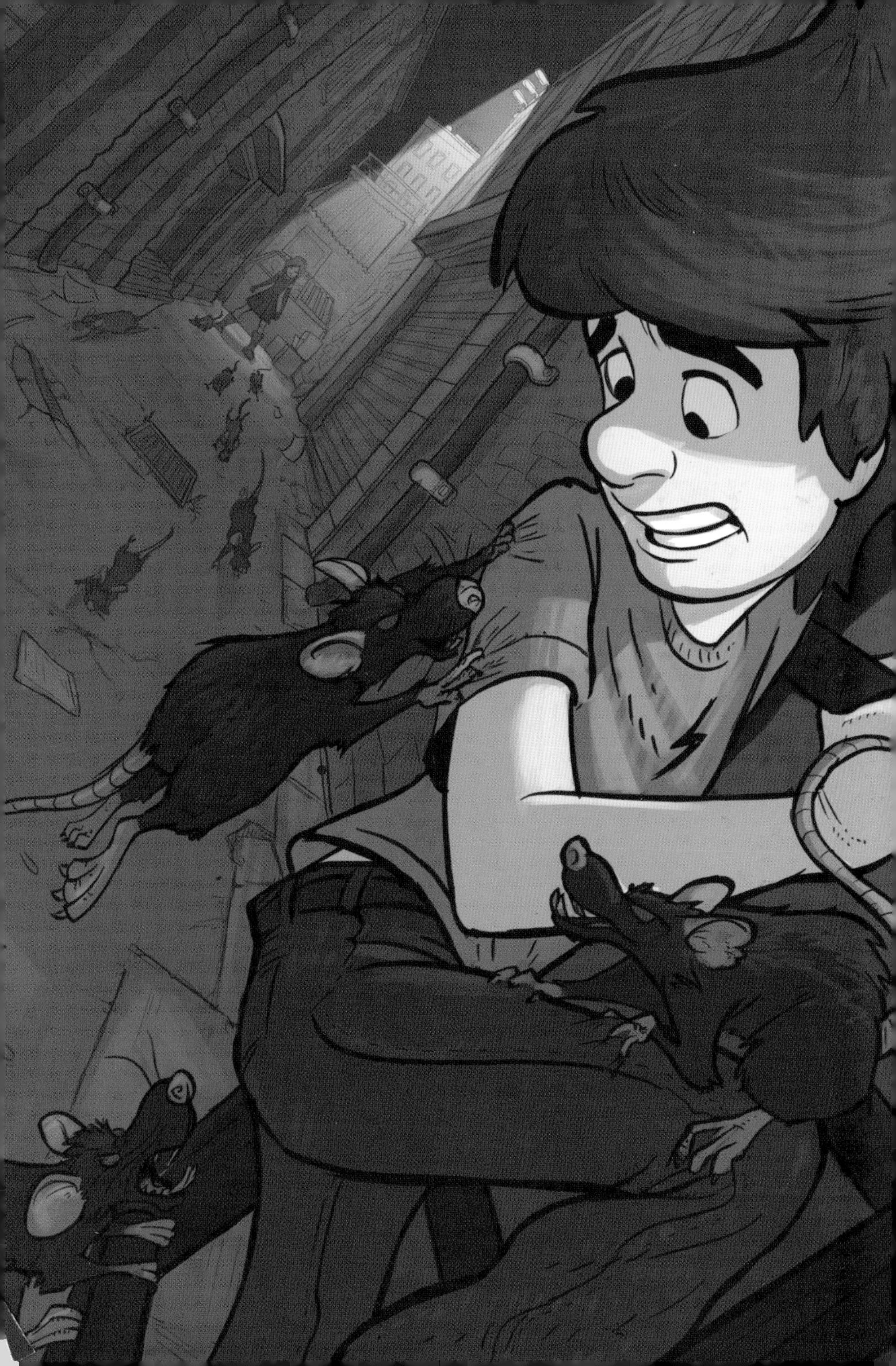

By the time I got the rats off me, a flock of pigeons had already surrounded Debbie and were carrying her away.

If she talked to me like that, I'd poop on her, too.

The Night Owl tried to get me to fly after her, but there was no way I was going through that again. Besides, I didn't have to follow her to know how to find her.

CHAPTER NINE

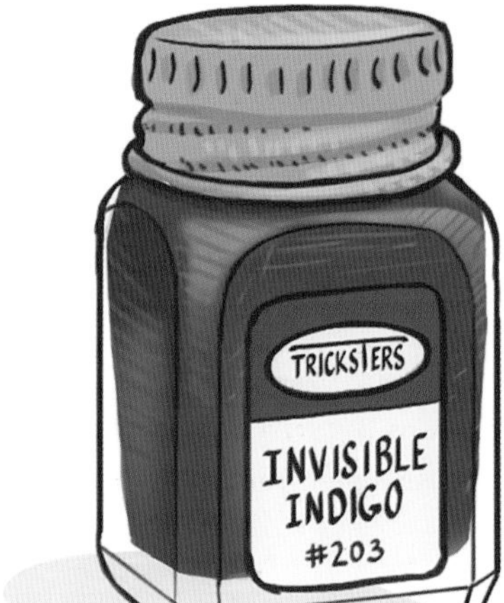
TRICKSTERS
INVISIBLE INDIGO
#203

Kirby is a kid who lives a few blocks away from me and has been obsessed with Debbie since third grade. And when I say obsessed, I mean *obsessed!*

Of course, Kirby acted like he didn't know where she was when I asked. But I knew better. As soon as I mentioned The Man With No Name, Kirby freaked out and did the worst thing he could have done: he activated his powers.

He ran out of his house, and one second he was there and the next he was gone. He has the power to turn invisible, so catching him was going to be a nightmare.

Thankfully, Kirby splashed through a puddle so The Night Owl, Lewis, and I were able to follow his footprints. He ran across some grass, though, and we lost him after that—until the library doors seemed to open up all by themselves.

I don't really recommend chasing someone through a library . . .

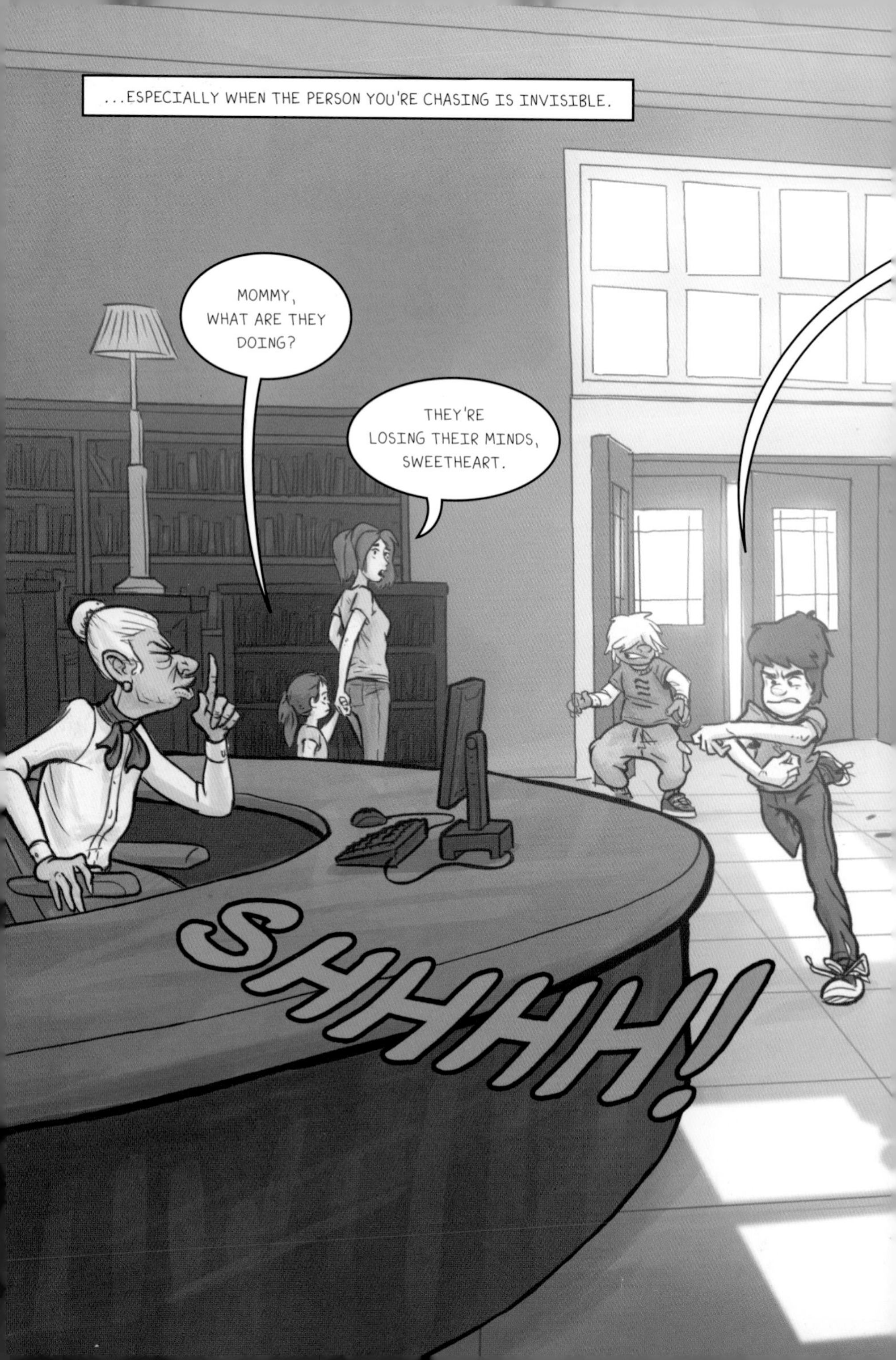
...ESPECIALLY WHEN THE PERSON YOU'RE CHASING IS INVISIBLE.
MOMMY, WHAT ARE THEY DOING?
THEY'RE LOSING THEIR MINDS, SWEETHEART.
SHHHH!

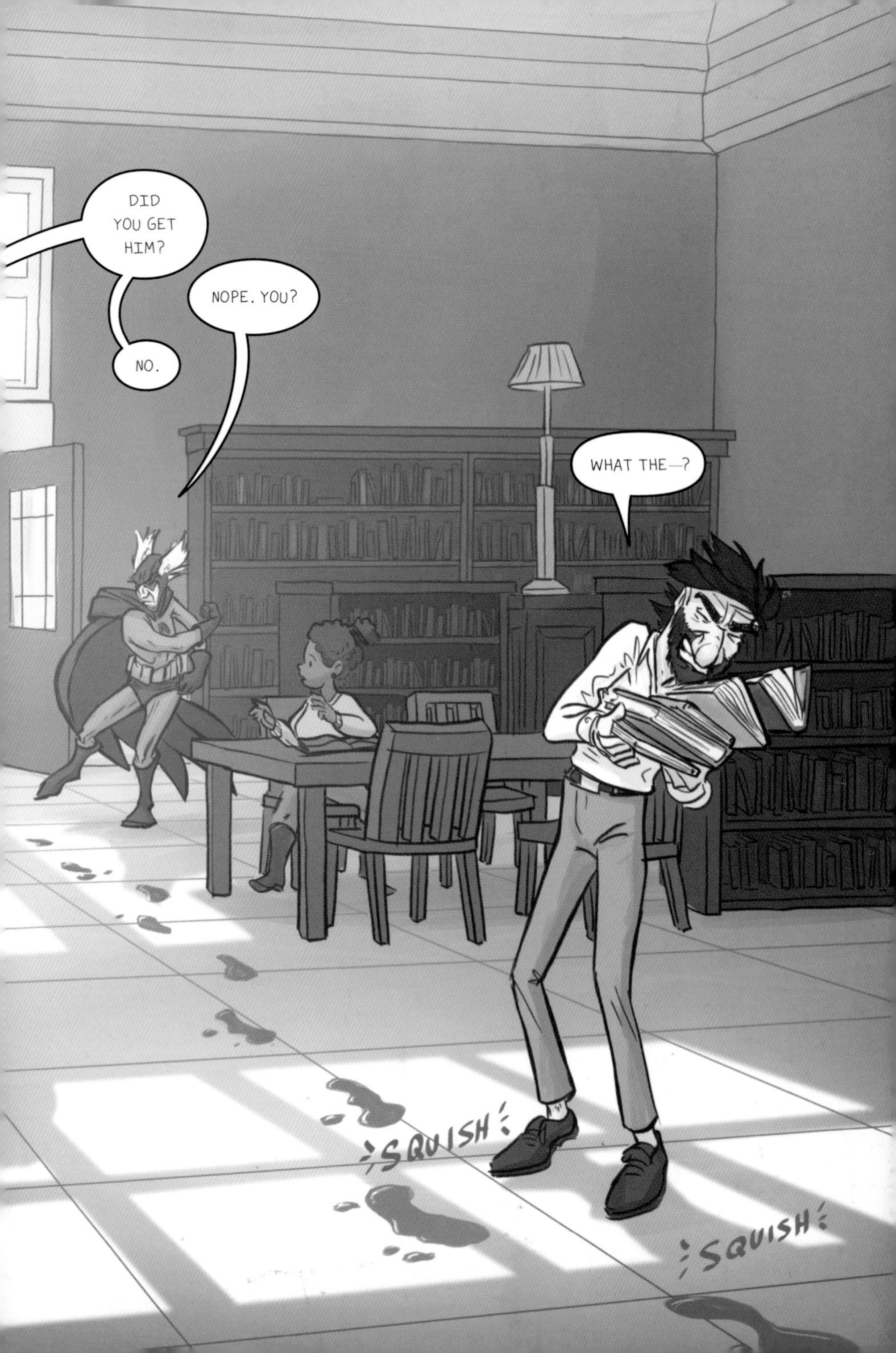
DID YOU GET HIM?
NOPE. YOU?
NO.
WHAT THE—?
SQUISH
SQUISH

The bathroom door swung open by itself and we knew we had him.

Unfortunately, it was the girls' bathroom.

We flailed our arms around like maniacs, but couldn't catch him. Then I remembered Kirby's defect.

It took a few seconds, but the room went totally silent ... except for Kirby's whistling boogers!

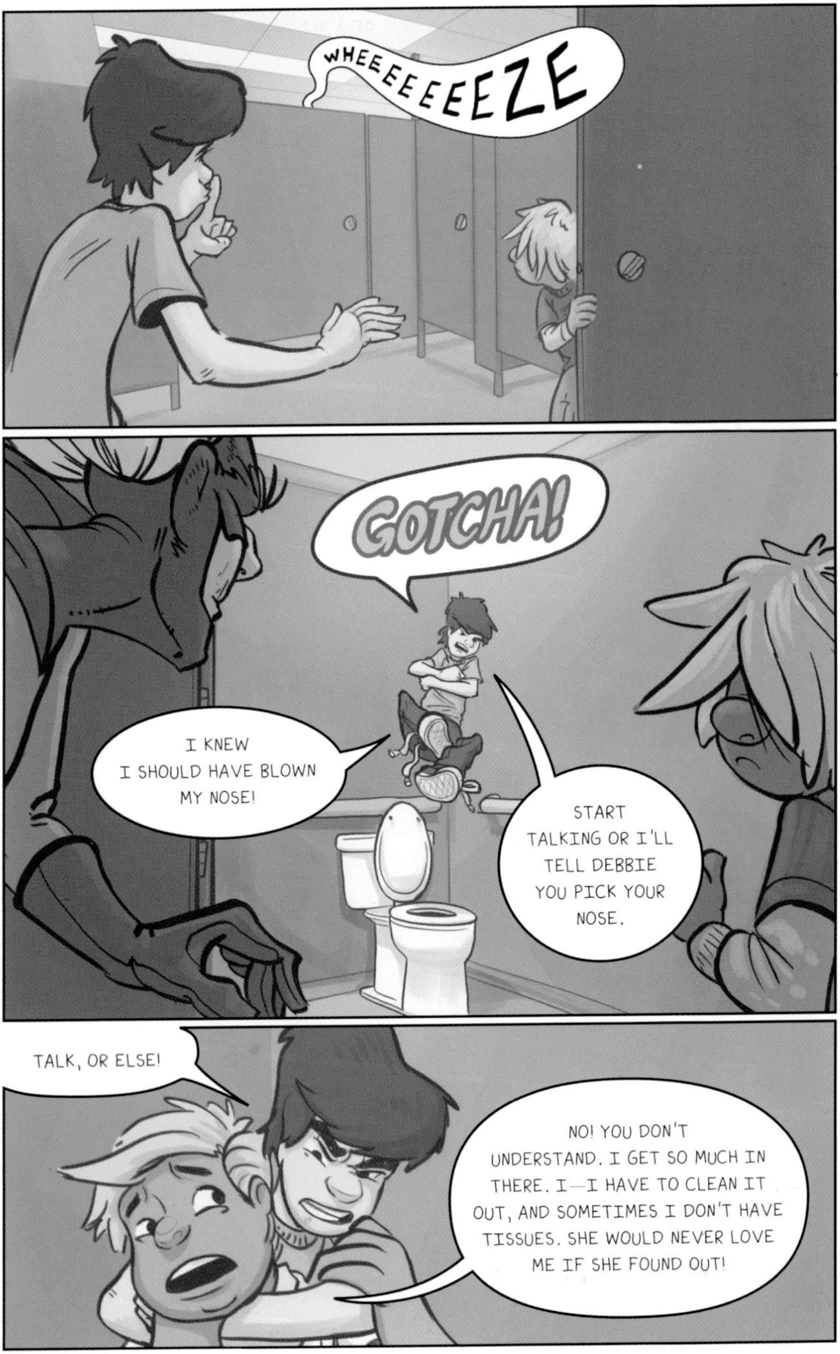
WHEEEEEEEEZE
GOTCHA!
I KNEW I SHOULD HAVE BLOWN MY NOSE!
START TALKING OR I'LL TELL DEBBIE YOU PICK YOUR NOSE.
TALK, OR ELSE!
NO! YOU DON'T UNDERSTAND. I GET SO MUCH IN THERE. I—I HAVE TO CLEAN IT OUT, AND SOMETIMES I DON'T HAVE TISSUES. SHE WOULD NEVER LOVE ME IF SHE FOUND OUT!

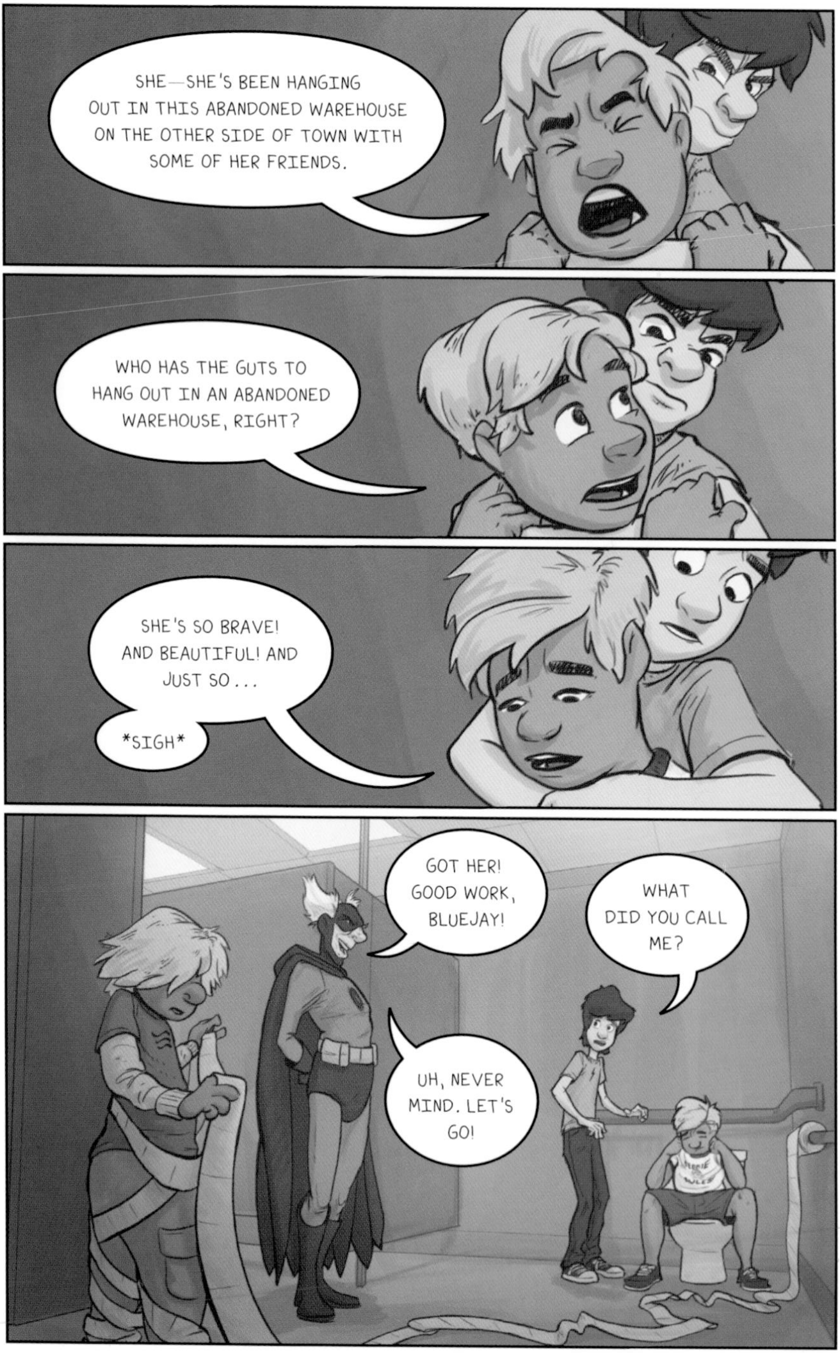
SHE—SHE'S BEEN HANGING OUT IN THIS ABANDONED WAREHOUSE ON THE OTHER SIDE OF TOWN WITH SOME OF HER FRIENDS.
WHO HAS THE GUTS TO HANG OUT IN AN ABANDONED WAREHOUSE, RIGHT?
SHE'S SO BRAVE! AND BEAUTIFUL! AND JUST SO . . .
SIGH
GOT HER! GOOD WORK, BLUEJAY!
WHAT DID YOU CALL ME?
UH, NEVER MIND. LET'S GO!

We took off, or at least we tried to.

Once we got the car going, then we had to search a million abandoned warehouses before we found the right one. The building was full of raccoons and opossums, so we knew were on the right track.

We snuck inside, and sure enough, we found Debbie.

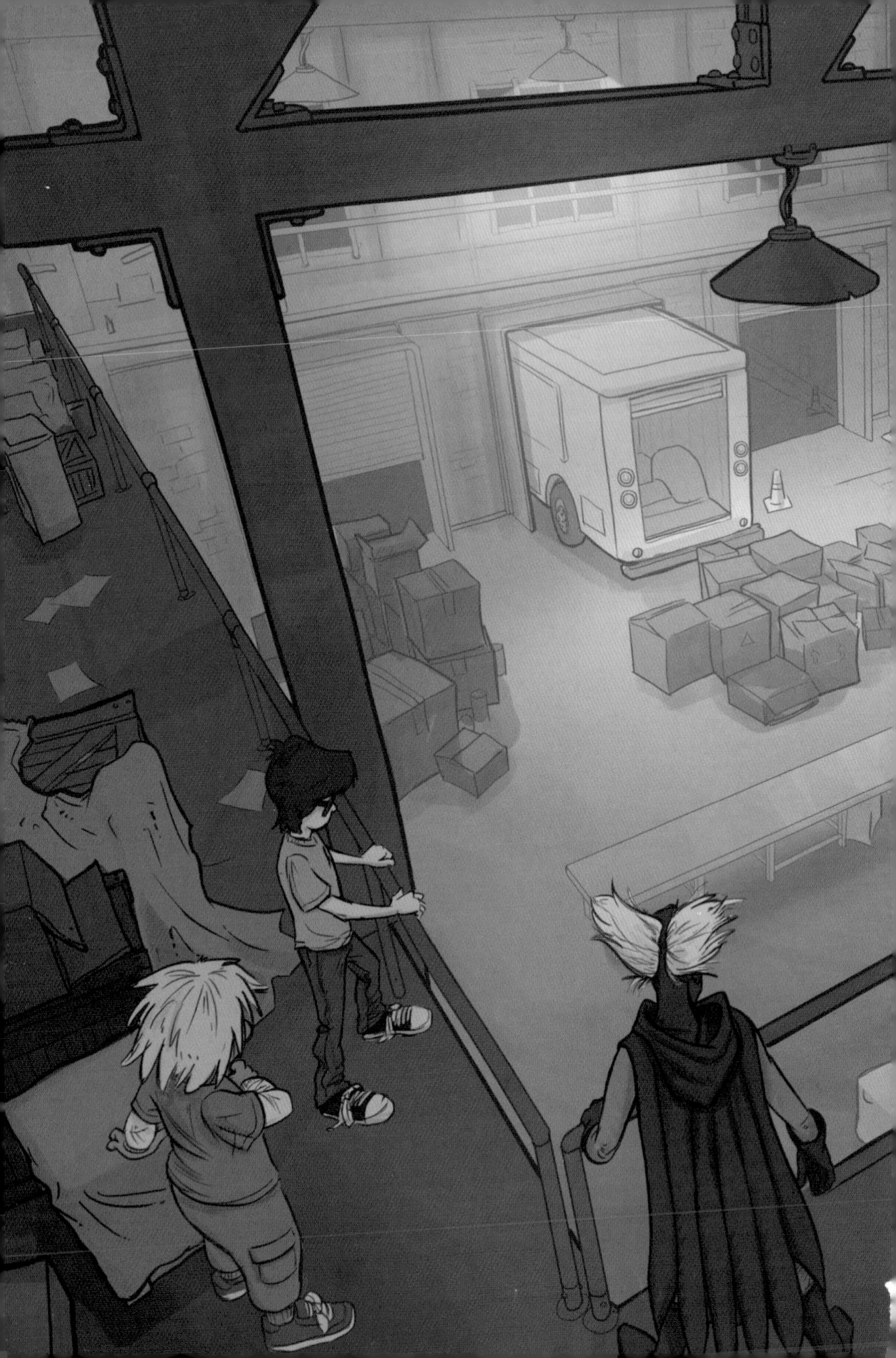

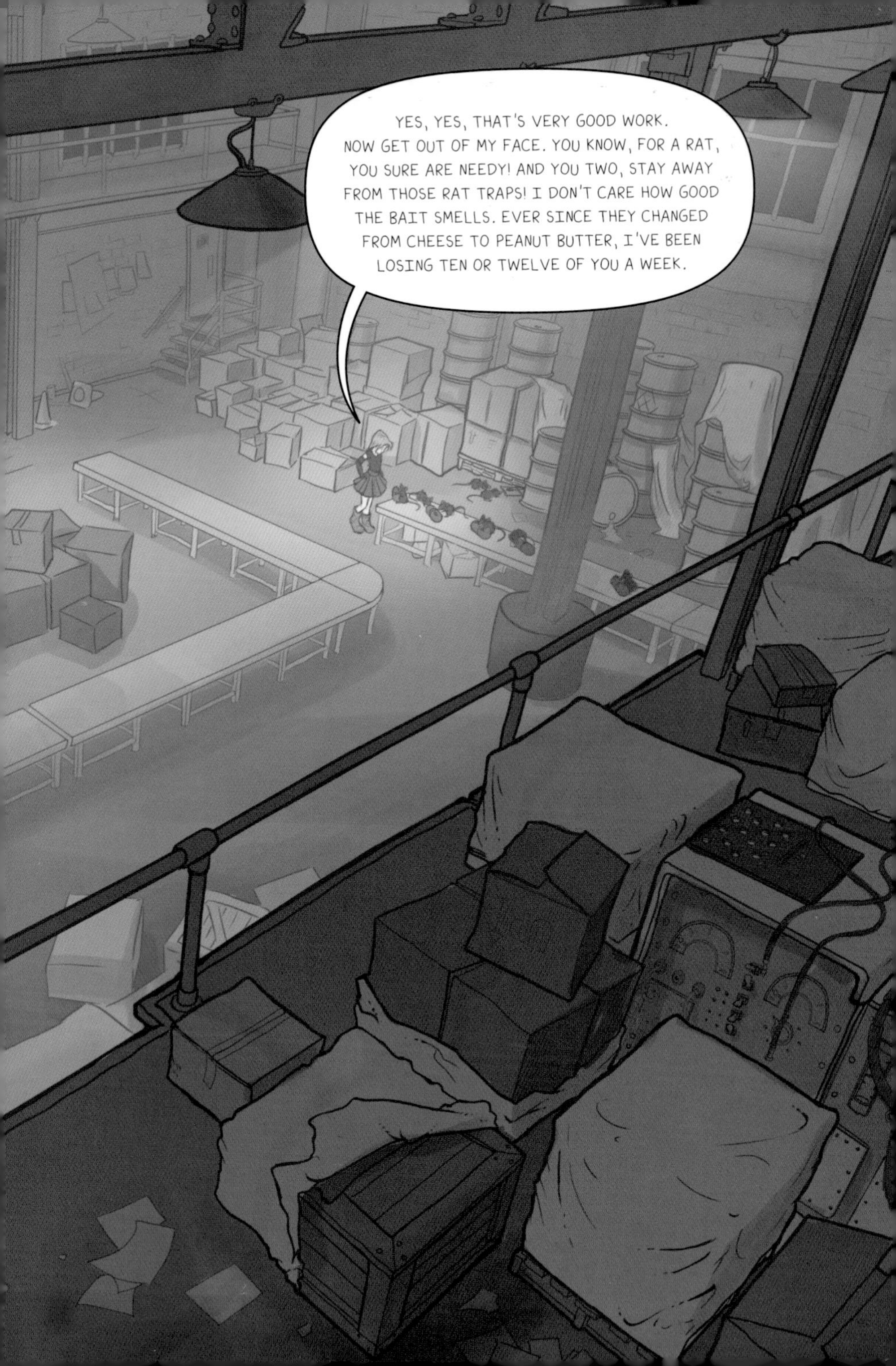
YES, YES, THAT'S VERY GOOD WORK. NOW GET OUT OF MY FACE. YOU KNOW, FOR A RAT, YOU SURE ARE NEEDY! AND YOU TWO, STAY AWAY FROM THOSE RAT TRAPS! I DON'T CARE HOW GOOD THE BAIT SMELLS. EVER SINCE THEY CHANGED FROM CHEESE TO PEANUT BUTTER, I'VE BEEN LOSING TEN OR TWELVE OF YOU A WEEK.

The Night Owl just smiled.

You should have seen those rats scatter when he jumped down in the middle of them.

The Night Owl backed Debbie into a corner, and boy, did he mean business. He was going to do whatever it took to get her to talk.

She was just about to crack when the warehouse doors flew open.

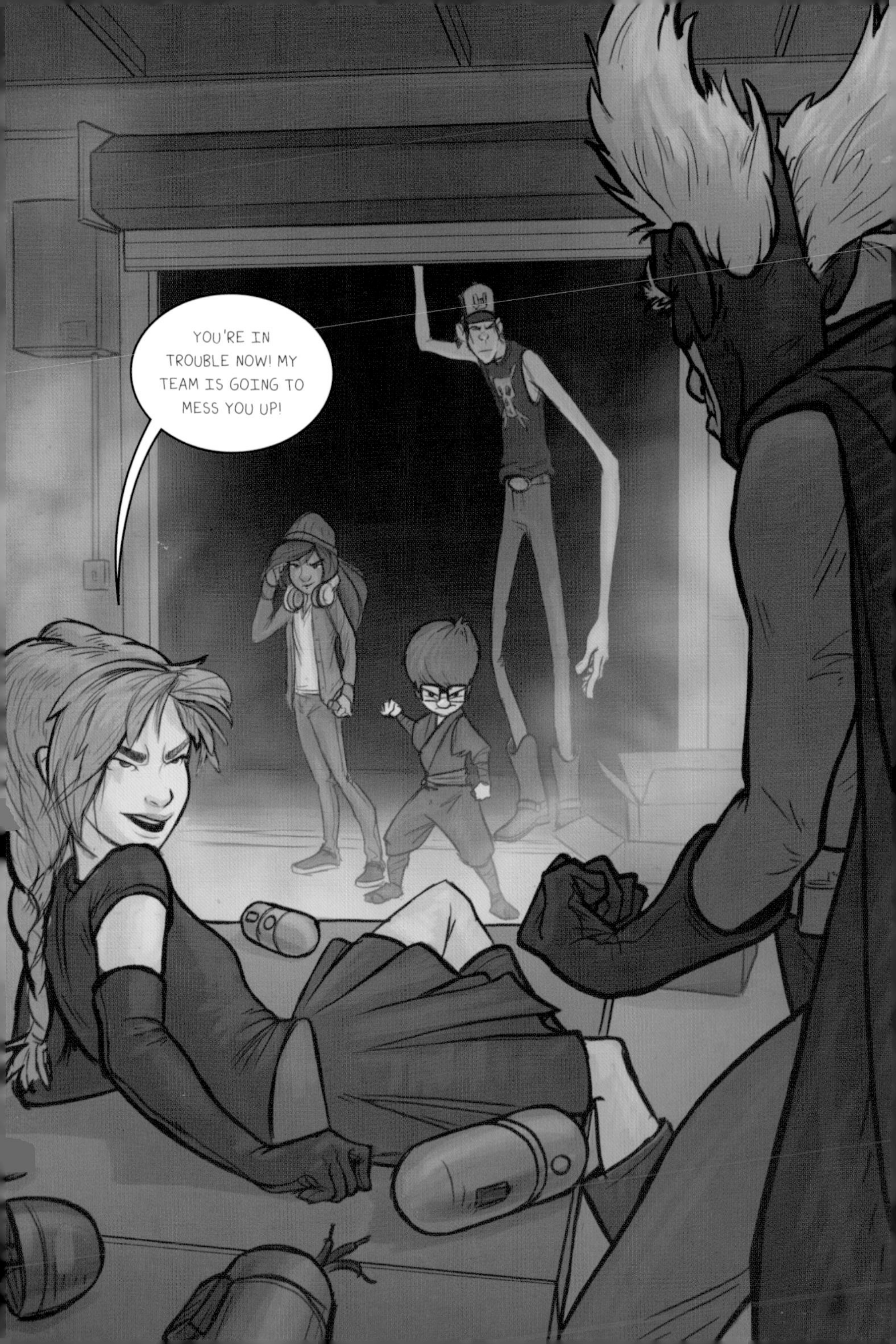
YOU'RE IN TROUBLE NOW! MY TEAM IS GOING TO MESS YOU UP!

I knew these kids. The girl was Tracy Giles. She used to live a few blocks from me. We had history together. Everyone calls her Squeak because she has a super-powered voice and her scream is so strong she can knock over a house . . .

...UNTIL HER ASTHMA KICKS IN.

Putty was a year older than me, but we still had a couple classes together. That should tell you what kind of student he was. You'd think, with his powers, he'd get really good grades because he can stretch out his body really, really far.

But when he stretches out like that, it takes a long time to shrink back to normal.

CHEATING AGAIN, WERE WE? I'LL SEE YOU IN DETENTION!

I didn't recognize the kid in the pajamas.

Lewis and I were getting covered in Putty's disgusting arm sweat, and
he was squeezing us pretty hard, too.

I couldn't use my lasers to get Putty off me because I didn't want to ruin my glasses so I did what anyone would do if they were wrapped up in a stinky, super-powered elastic arm.

I WIPED OFF THE SWEAT AND GAVE HIM AN ERASER BURN (A.K.A. A SNAKE BITE)!

OWWW

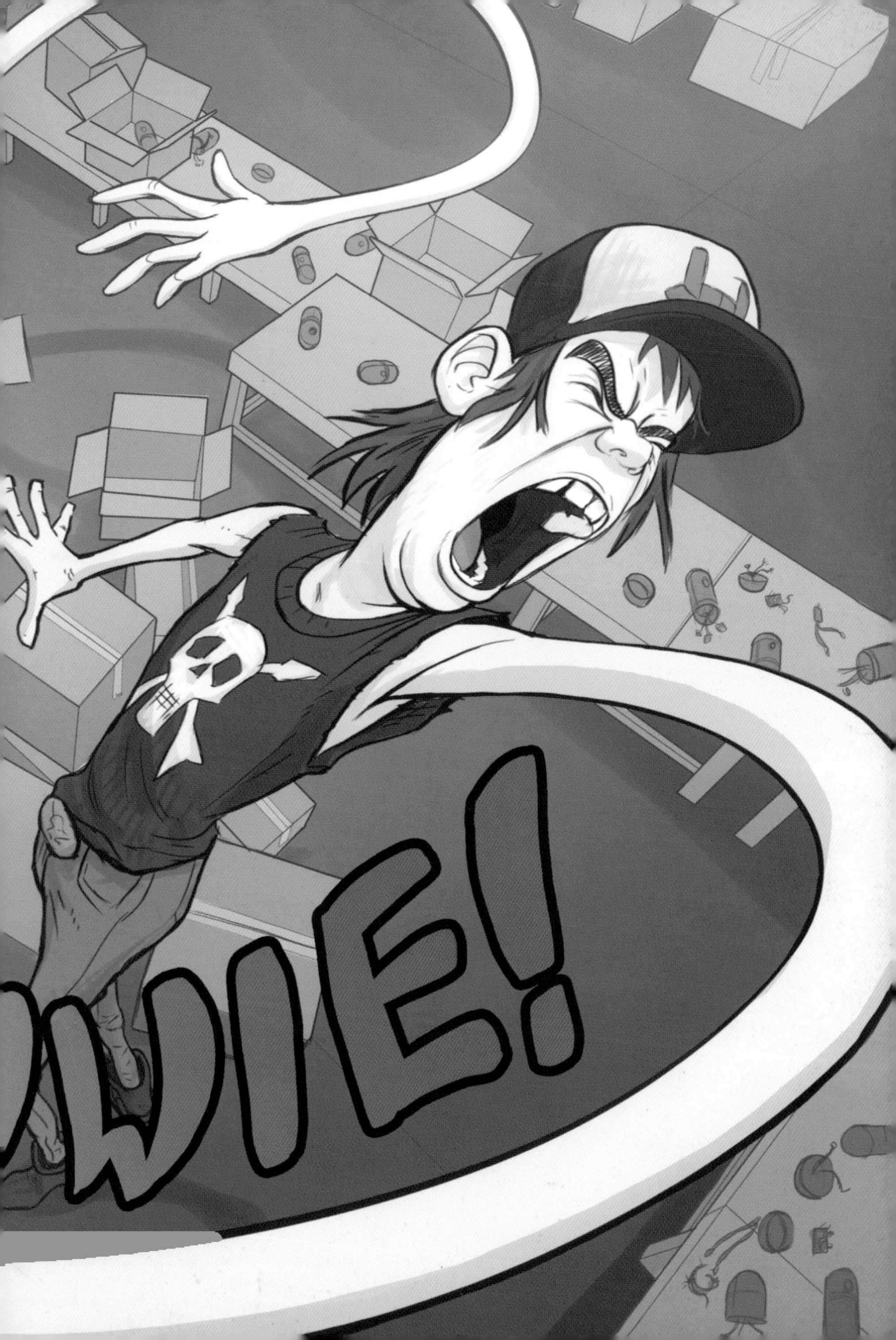
WIE!

Just then, the ninja kid turned around and chucked about a million throwing stars.

Thankfully, he threw them at a poster . . .

The Night Owl kept harassing Debbie for answers. Without her rats to help her, she had to think on her feet. And let me tell you, what she did was as genius as it was disgusting.

The Night Owl tried to use one of his gadgets on the ninja, but it was so old and crusty that it was pretty much useless. So he threw it at him instead. It hit the kid right in the head.

I guess he didn't see it coming.

Putty's arm had already gone limp, so he used it as a whip, and Squeak got enough breath back to scream at me again. I hit the ground so hard, I almost cracked my head open on the cement and my lasers went crazy. Well, crazier than usual.

AND I WAS HAVING A GOOD HAIR DAY!

Lewis had said what Putty was thinking, so the ninja kid thought he had accidentally attacked the wrong person. The ninja teleported away from Lewis and ended up double-punching Squeak in the kidneys!

It was chaos—the kind of awesome chaos you only read about in comic books.

Until Putty almost got us all killed.

We booked it out of there as fast as we could, which was tough since one of us was about two hundred years old.

We got out of there just in time.

Just so you know, jumping out of a building that's exploding isn't as awesome as it looks in the movies. My ears were ringing so bad, I couldn't hear anything for hours. I don't recommend it.

CHAPTER TEN

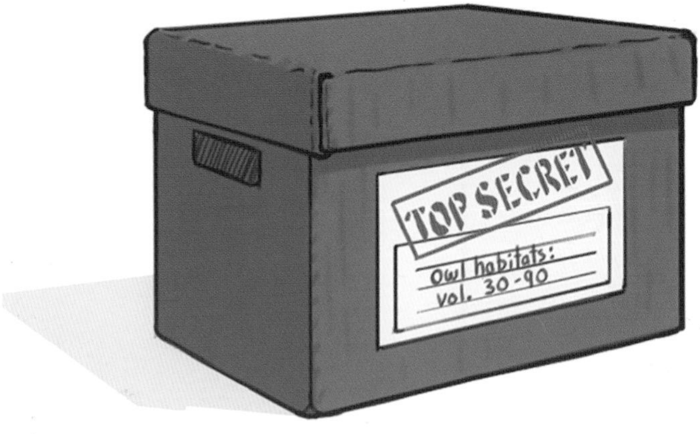
TOP SECRET
Owl habitats:
vol. 30-90

For the third time in a row, the bad guys had gotten away. What made things even worse was we didn't really have any more clues to help us track them down, with the warehouse being blown to bits and all.

The Night Owl told us he kept all the data he had collected on The Man With No Name back at his hideout, so we piled into the car and headed out.

MAYBE WE CAN FIND SOMETHING IN MY FILES THAT'LL HELP US GET BACK ON TRACK.

OH, HERE WE ARE. OKAY BOYS, CLOSE YOUR EYES. I'VE GOT TO KEEP THIS LOCATION A SECRET.

I was really hoping the inside would be a bit more impressive.

It wasn't.

Have you ever seen the shows on TV about those hoarders who never throw anything away for years and years and they end up collecting so much stuff that you can't even see the carpet anymore and they have to climb over piles of magazines and old clothes just to get into their houses? That's pretty much what the inside of The Night Owl's house looked like, only worse.

Finding anything in that mess looked impossible to me.

We got to work searching through The Night Owl's files, but I ended up doing most of the work.

I called my mom and told her I would be staying at Lewis's house again tonight. She, of course, responded like I knew she would.

After about twenty minutes of going through The Night Owl's files, I was going bonkers and needed to take a break. I wanted to watch TV, but if The Night Owl even had a TV, I'd never be able to find it under all his trash. Besides, it would probably be some super old TV that only played shows in black and white.

I had to find something else to occupy my time. I went into the bathroom and filled a bowl with warm water. My plan was to prank The Night Owl by putting his hand in the water to make him wet his pants, but I think he beat me to the punch....

While The Night Owl caught up on his beauty sleep and Lewis worked on his Picassos, I got back to work going through the papers. I found an address book underneath a stack of folders and went through all of The Man With No Name's old allies, but most of the supervillains he had teamed up with in the past were either dead or too old to even remember their own names.

WHO IS THIS?

SPEAK UP!

OH, I SEE!
THE MAN WITH NO WHAT NOW?
I KNEW A MAN WITH NO
TOES. THE TOELESS TERROR. HE HAD
BIG FEET DESPITE THE
FACT HE DIDN'T HAVE ANY TOES.
HE WORE A SIZE 13 SHOE
BUT REFUSED TO WEAR ANYTHING
BUT SANDALS.

WHY, I REMEMBER
ONE NIGHT AFTER DEFEATING SOME
SUPERHEROES, HE AND I FOUND
AN OLD VENTRILOQUIST DUMMY BEHIND
A DUMPSTER. WE GRABBED A COUPLE
OF WIGS AND AN ANT FARM
AND WE...

This was getting us nowhere. All we really knew at this point was that The Man With No Name was using Defectives to build bombs. We had no idea where he was going to set it off or when he was going to do it. If we were going to stop him from blowing up innocent people, we were running out of time.

Then it happened.

The paper Lewis was drawing on had a list of all the items stolen by the guys from Henchmen, Inc. over the last few months: a totem pole, some arrowheads, a few horseshoes. At first glance, it looked like a bunch of random stuff. But then it hit me. They all had one thing in common.

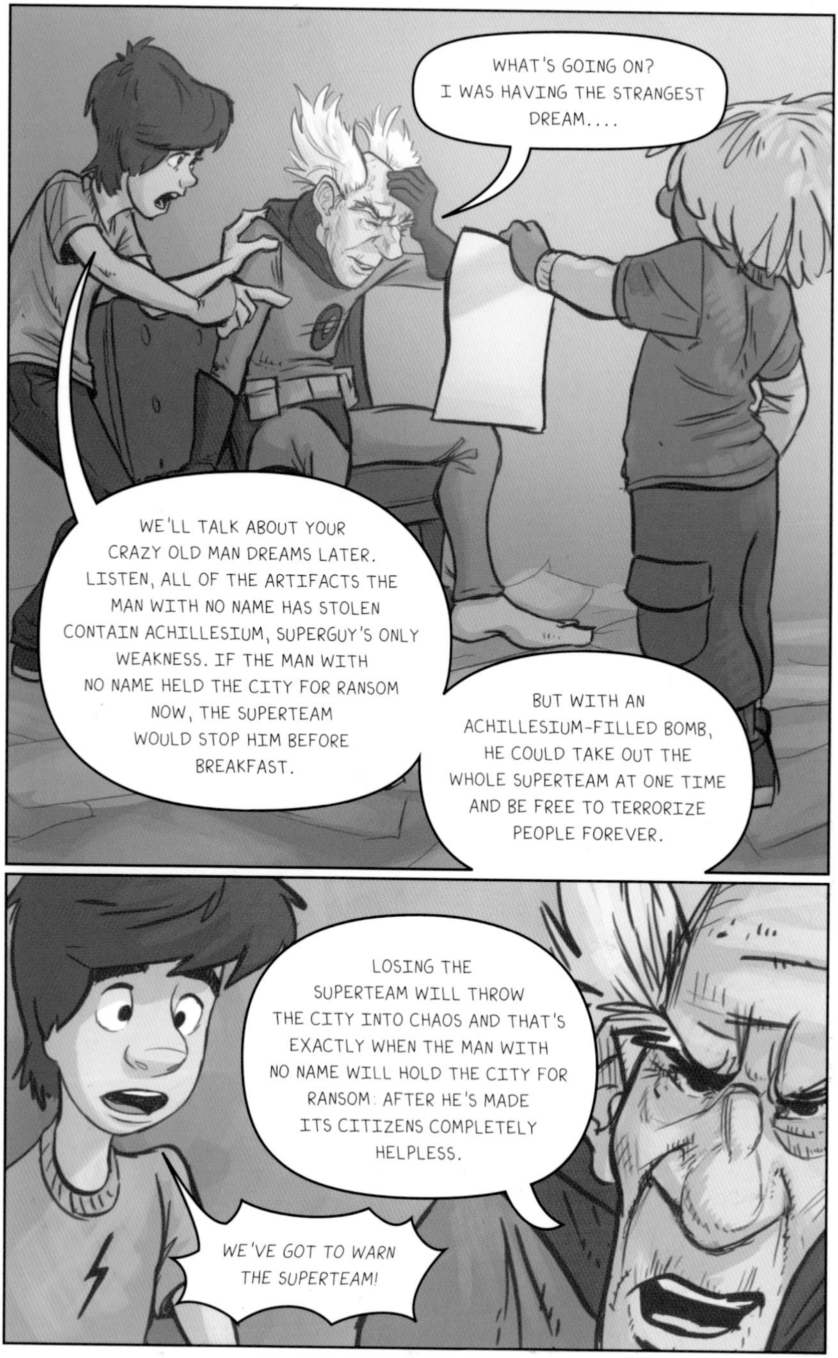
WHAT'S GOING ON? I WAS HAVING THE STRANGEST DREAM....
WE'LL TALK ABOUT YOUR CRAZY OLD MAN DREAMS LATER. LISTEN, ALL OF THE ARTIFACTS THE MAN WITH NO NAME HAS STOLEN CONTAIN ACHILLESIUM, SUPERGUY'S ONLY WEAKNESS. IF THE MAN WITH NO NAME HELD THE CITY FOR RANSOM NOW, THE SUPERTEAM WOULD STOP HIM BEFORE BREAKFAST.
BUT WITH AN ACHILLESIUM-FILLED BOMB, HE COULD TAKE OUT THE WHOLE SUPERTEAM AT ONE TIME AND BE FREE TO TERRORIZE PEOPLE FOREVER.
LOSING THE SUPERTEAM WILL THROW THE CITY INTO CHAOS AND THAT'S EXACTLY WHEN THE MAN WITH NO NAME WILL HOLD THE CITY FOR RANSOM: AFTER HE'S MADE ITS CITIZENS COMPLETELY HELPLESS.
WE'VE GOT TO WARN THE SUPERTEAM!

Unfortunately, the Superteam wasn't as willing to listen as we'd hoped.

Superguy laughed and went on and on about how he was leader of the best superhero team in the world and how nothing went on in the city without them knowing about it and that's why the city didn't have any other superheroes protecting it. And if this bomb were a real threat, the Superteam would already know about it, because they were so perfect, blah, blah, blah.

Then he did the worst thing ever in the history of anything.

The whole Superteam laughed at me. Superguy, Led Zapplin, Lycanine, Hydratia, Trevor—all of them laughed at *me* in front of the whole world.

So in about thirty seconds, my idols managed to humiliate me in front of millions of people, ruining my life forever.

When Superguy finally put me down, I ran off the stage.

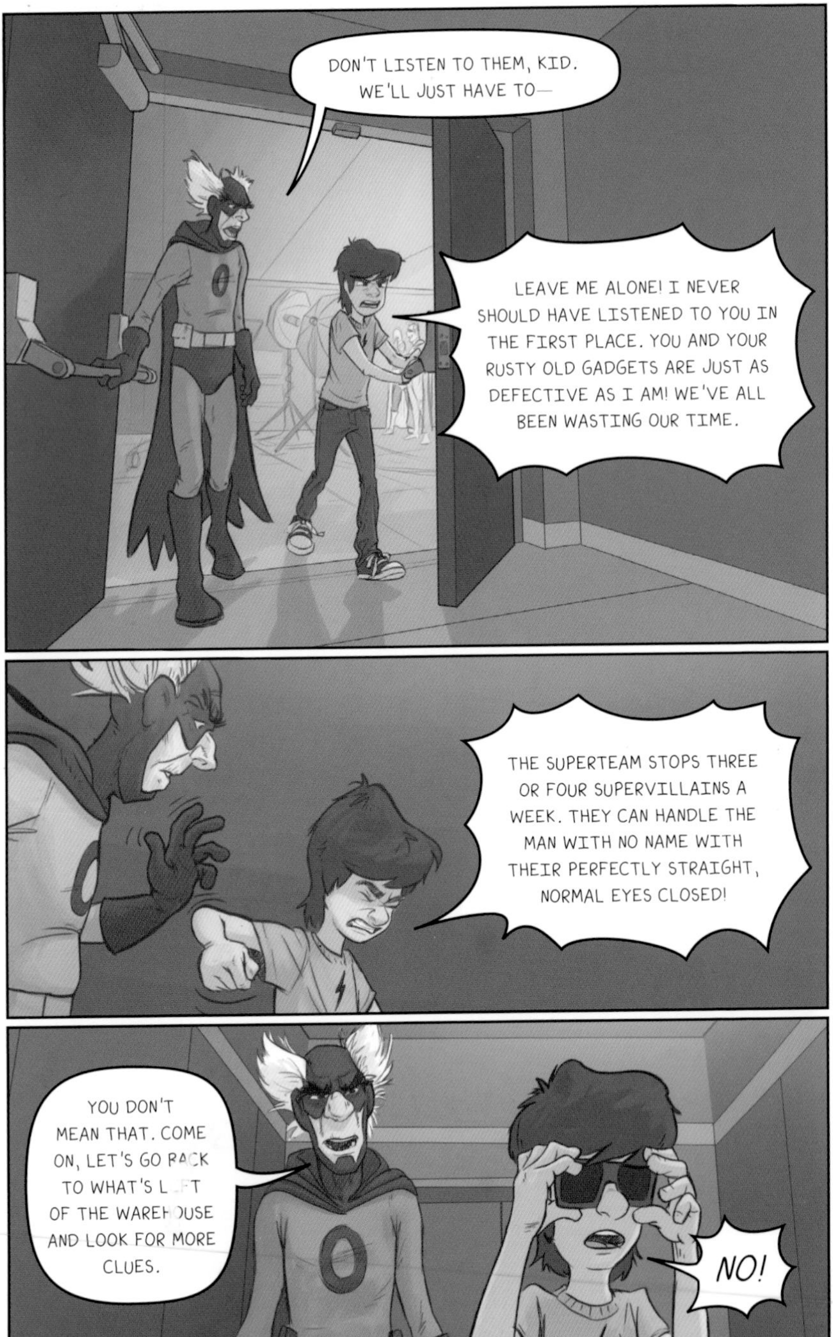
DON'T LISTEN TO THEM, KID. WE'LL JUST HAVE TO—
LEAVE ME ALONE! I NEVER SHOULD HAVE LISTENED TO YOU IN THE FIRST PLACE. YOU AND YOUR RUSTY OLD GADGETS ARE JUST AS DEFECTIVE AS I AM! WE'VE ALL BEEN WASTING OUR TIME.
THE SUPERTEAM STOPS THREE OR FOUR SUPERVILLAINS A WEEK. THEY CAN HANDLE THE MAN WITH NO NAME WITH THEIR PERFECTLY STRAIGHT, NORMAL EYES CLOSED!
YOU DON'T MEAN THAT. COME ON, LET'S GO BACK TO WHAT'S LEFT OF THE WAREHOUSE AND LOOK FOR MORE CLUES.
NO!

When I got home, though, I was in a lot of trouble. My parents thought I was going to be at Lewis's house all day, but they had just seen me on the news. The minute I walked through the door, my dad grounded me.

So it was official. My entire life was ruined.

CHAPTER
ELEVEN

When I got up the next day, my parents had already gone to work, so I sat down to play some video games to take my mind off how much my life stunk. If my parents were home, they would have freaked out—video games were the first thing they took away when they grounded me.

I wasn't getting away with anything, though, because apparently my sister/sisters decided to hide some water balloons in my console, which was now soaking wet!

So I turned on the TV.

Because my parents were working, I was in charge of my sister/sisters. There were only three of them today, thankfully. I got them dressed and was feeding them breakfast when The Night Owl showed up at our back door.

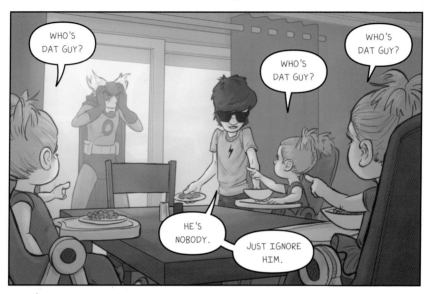

That's exactly what I was trying to do: ignore him.

But he wouldn't go away.

I finally opened the door and was going to let The Night Owl have a piece of my mind . . .

Then he walked away.

I climbed the stairs to my room and pulled my "costume" out of my backpack. Maybe The Night Owl was right. The Superteam didn't even think The Man With No Name existed, so they definitely weren't going to do anything to stop him. Lewis, The Night Owl, and I were the only ones taking this threat seriously, and if anyone was going to stop The Man With No Name, it would have to be us.

But finding him seemed impossible. Debbie knew we were after her, so she wasn't going to show her face again; Putty dropped out of school last year, so I had no idea how to find him; I had never met the ninja kid before; and I hadn't seen Squeak outside of class since she moved. How the heck were we supposed to track down The Man With No Name?

Then it hit me: I had just answered my own question! Debbie, Putty, and Squeak had all gone to my school.

I ran to my desk and grabbed my yearbook. Just past the team sports section, I found what I was looking for.

Our yearbook had two-page collages dedicated to each teacher with photos of their students from past years. And there they were: Putty, Squeak, Ninja, and Debbie, all in one spot. And right smack in the middle of them was our history teacher, Mr. Disher.

The man we'd been searching for all along had been under my nose the whole time! Mr. Disher was obviously The Man With No Name, and he had created a team of supervillains out of the Defective students he had taught in his history class over the years. If he had teamed up with any *real* villains, the Superteam would have known about it, and they would have been all over him like head lice on Putty. But no one would suspect that Mr. Disher would create a team out of Defectives, because no one expected Defectives to ever amount to anything.

For a second, I wondered why he never asked me to join his crew. I would never have gone along with his plan, of course, but still. He didn't even ask.

Was I really so defective that I wasn't even good enough to be asked to join a team of Defectives? Well, I was going to show Mr. Disher, a.k.a. The Man With No Name, what a Defective like me could really do.

CHAPTER
TWELVE

Lewis, The Night Owl, and I got to the school building right as the sun was setting. The summer school students had already gone home for the day.

But Mr. Disher's classroom light was still on.

UNTIL THE NIGHT OWL TOOK IT OUT WITH AN OWLARANG!

The old man seriously needs a new name for his gadgets. I mean, Owlarang sounds like a cross between an owl and an orangutan.

THAT WOULD BE A DANGEROUS COMBINATION BECAUSE OWLS CAN SEE REALLY FAR AND PRIMATES ARE KNOWN TO FLING POO.

SPLAT.

EWW! WHO THREW THAT?

The second the lights went out, the three of us jumped into the room to get the drop on The Man With No Name, but instead, the bad guys got the drop on us.

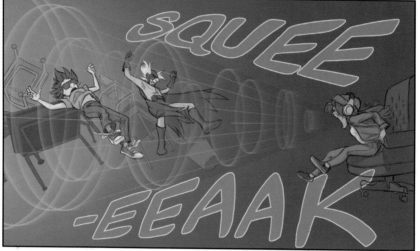

Squeak screamed so hard, she blew a hole through the wall, and we flew through it, landing in the quad.

Mr. Disher must have known we were coming. Before we could even get off the floor, Putty stretched his arms and punched each of us in the face. All he really had to do was put his lice-filled head near mine and I would have gone running.

The Night Owl threw some more Owlarangs at Squeak, and she had to scream again to stop them from pinning her to the wall.

Which was pretty smart of him, because even though none of them hit her, she ran out of breath.

Putty came up behind the three of us and wrapped his arms around our necks. I looked down at his elbow and fired my lasers, which was a mistake.

I hit The Night Owl's utility belt by accident and half his gadgets went off!

Putty laughed so hard he almost let us go . . .

...but then the whole utility belt caught on fire.

I would have probably laughed, too, if I didn't have Putty's sweaty arm crushing me to death. My head got really fuzzy and my vision was going dark.

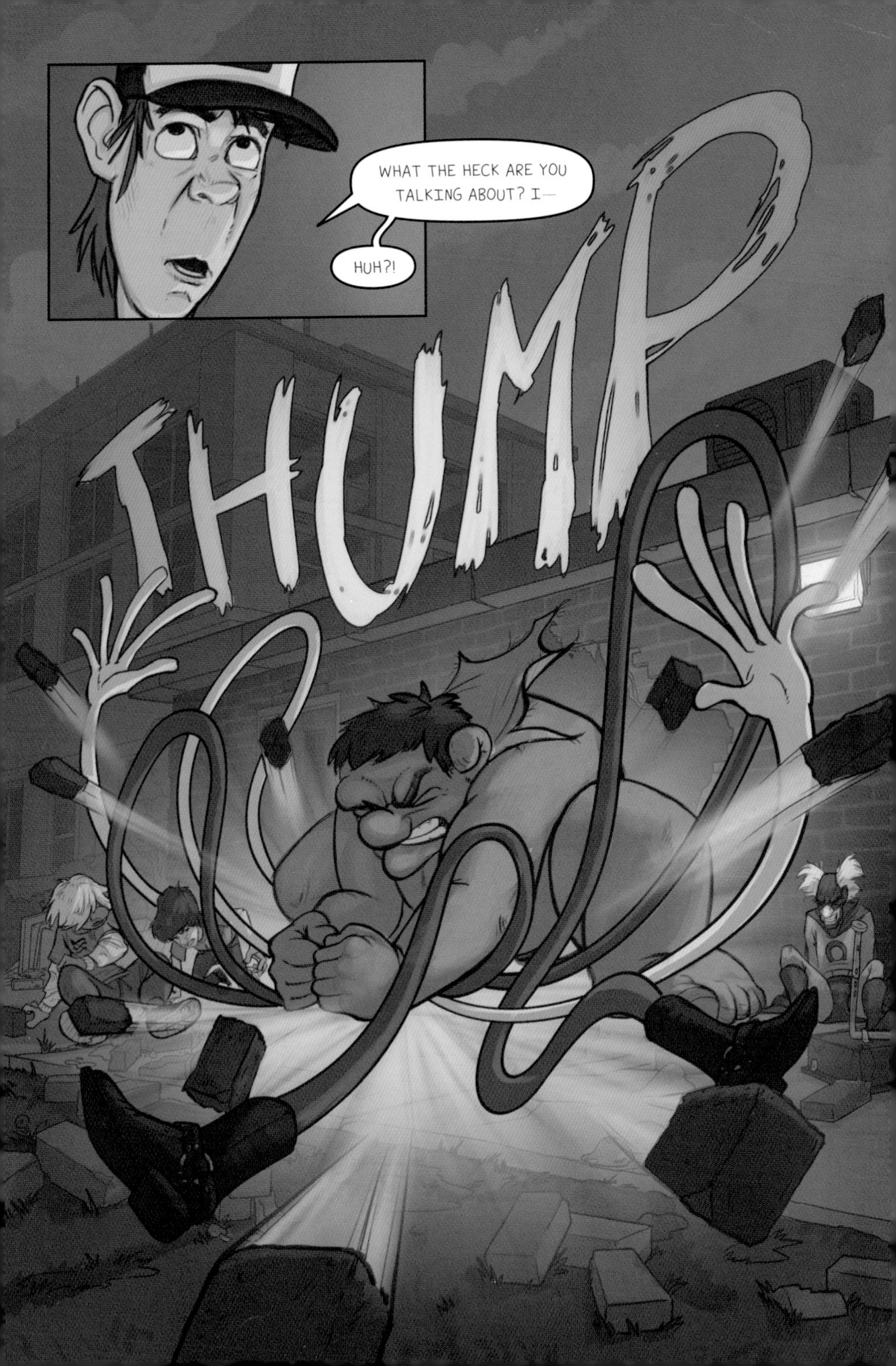
WHAT THE HECK ARE YOU TALKING ABOUT? I—
HUH?!
THUMP

It was perfect timing!

I had sent a message to Tim and Crash earlier, hoping they would come help us, but I hadn't ever heard back. I guess they got the message, which I was really happy about at this particular moment.

Squeak freaked when she saw Tim turn Putty into ...um, putty. She took a breath from her inhaler and screamed us into another wall. She hit us so hard even Tim fell down.

Then there was Crash.

Squeak went all Big Bad Wolf on Crash, but her power didn't work on him. Crash couldn't turn or stop without falling over, but he could run a straight line just fine.

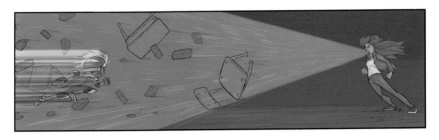

You should have seen Squeak's face when Crash sprinted through her scream and grabbed her inhaler!

Without that, Squeak was pretty much out of the game, and Putty was going to be a pile of goo for the next few hours. We tried to stop him from escaping, but he slipped down a drain and got away.

Squeak made a run for it, and Crash would have caught her if she hadn't turned a corner.

Once again, the bad guys had gotten away, but at least this time it was because we had finally beaten them.

Without any bad guys to question, we set out to look for more clues. Unfortunately, Mr. Disher had cleaned his classroom out. Every history book, every poster, every*thing* that might have even mentioned The Man With No Name was gone. He even took the poster from Trevor's end-of-the-year project.

I was glad that was gone. It was bad enough seeing Trevor on the news and hearing everyone at school talk about how great he was, but I had to sit in history class all semester with that poster and Mr. Disher's comments, "Very detailed" and "Excellent job," written across the front. The comments might as well have said, "You're better than Marshall at this, too!" I know that doesn't even make sense, because Trevor made the poster before I was in Mr. Disher's class, but the best comment I ever got from Mr. Disher was, "This made my cat cry."

Anyway, the police sirens in the distance were growing louder, and we knew we had to act fast. Like I said, pretty much everything in the classroom was gone, but we did find pieces of a torn-up photograph in the trash can. Many of the scraps look like they had been burned, but there were a few pieces that weren't completely destroyed.

Lewis grabbed them out of my hand and put the picture back together faster than I thought humanly possible. I'd have to remember he could do that the next time I broke one of my mom's glass vases.

It was tough to make out the photo when Lewis finished, but the picture was of Mr. Disher and one of his classes in front of the Big-Time Carnival a few years ago. They had gone there on a field trip because the Great Gator, one of the villains they talk about in our textbooks, was a sideshow at the carnival.

I wish he would have taken our class to the carnival. The only field trip we got to go on was to a factory that made the Superteam's capes.

Burning the photo didn't make any sense.

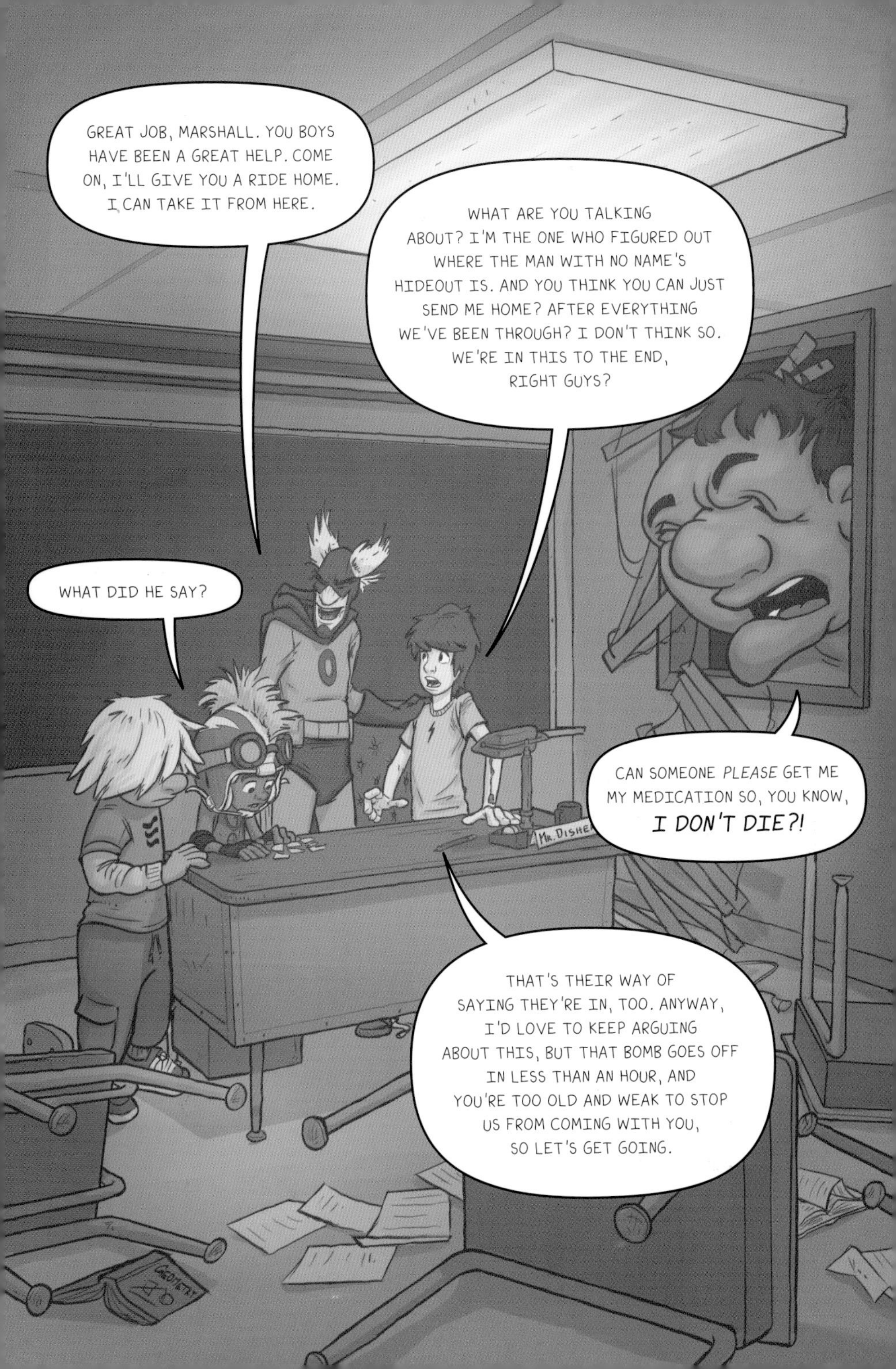
GREAT JOB, MARSHALL. YOU BOYS HAVE BEEN A GREAT HELP. COME ON, I'LL GIVE YOU A RIDE HOME. I CAN TAKE IT FROM HERE.
WHAT ARE YOU TALKING ABOUT? I'M THE ONE WHO FIGURED OUT WHERE THE MAN WITH NO NAME'S HIDEOUT IS. AND YOU THINK YOU CAN JUST SEND ME HOME? AFTER EVERYTHING WE'VE BEEN THROUGH? I DON'T THINK SO. WE'RE IN THIS TO THE END, RIGHT GUYS?
WHAT DID HE SAY?
CAN SOMEONE *PLEASE* GET ME MY MEDICATION SO, YOU KNOW, **I DON'T DIE?!**
THAT'S THEIR WAY OF SAYING THEY'RE IN, TOO. ANYWAY, I'D LOVE TO KEEP ARGUING ABOUT THIS, BUT THAT BOMB GOES OFF IN LESS THAN AN HOUR, AND YOU'RE TOO OLD AND WEAK TO STOP US FROM COMING WITH YOU, SO LET'S GET GOING.

CHAPTER THIRTEEN

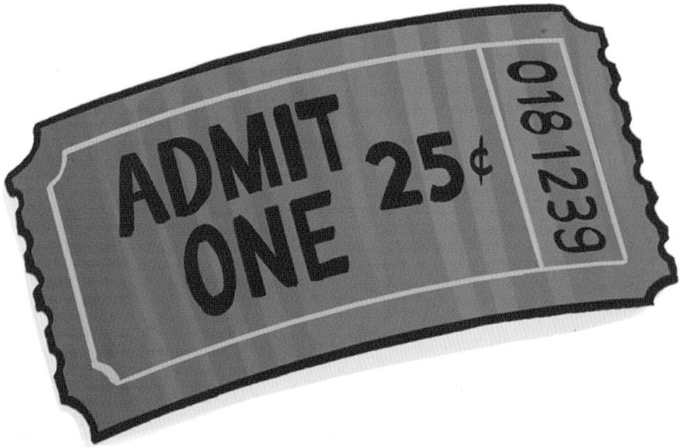
ADMIT ONE
25¢
0181239

I'm positive that we broke about a hundred traffic laws on the way to the carnival, but with the way The Night Owl drives, not wearing my seat belt wasn't one of them!

The Big-Time Carnival shut down about two months ago because the Superteam needed the lot to add another wing to their headquarters. The carnival was right next to their building, and I heard they wanted to tear it down to build a Superteam museum. They were even going to charge admission!

By the way, if you ever want to freak yourself out, forget going to one of those theme parks during Halloween where everyone dresses up like zombies and jumps out at you from behind a dark corner. Just go to an old carnival after all the lights go out. Yikes!

I stayed right in the middle of the group. I've seen enough horror movies to know the people at the back get eaten first and everything jumps out at the people in front.

I let Lewis lead the way this time.

Thankfully, we didn't have to wander around outside for very long. All the tents were dark except for the circus arena. We snuck over to one of the arena's windows to make sure we were at the right place. Sure enough, there was Mr. Disher, and he did not sound happy.

I was going to climb through the window but a rat came around the corner of the building just as Crash was about to give me a boost. We quickly plastered ourselves to the wall and held our breath.

NOBODY MOVE. THAT'S PROBABLY ONE OF DEBBIE'S RATS.

OF COURSE A PIECE OF THE PEANUT HAD TO COME OFF AND BOUNCE RIGHT TOWARD US.

I couldn't believe it hadn't noticed us yet.

UNTIL IT SAW THE NIGHT OWL'S SHADOW.

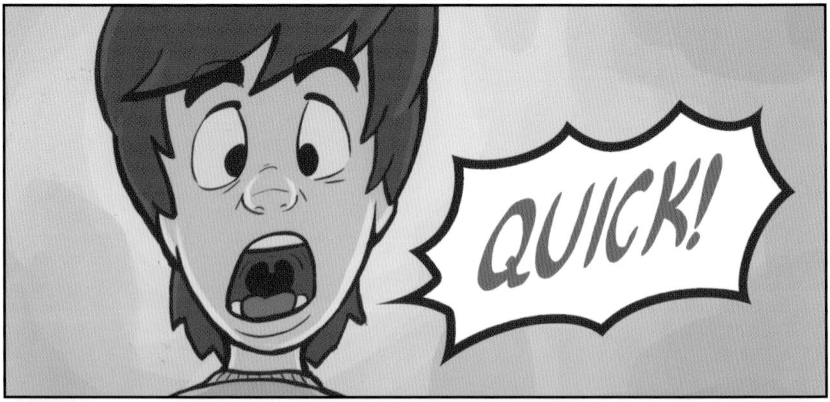
QUICK!

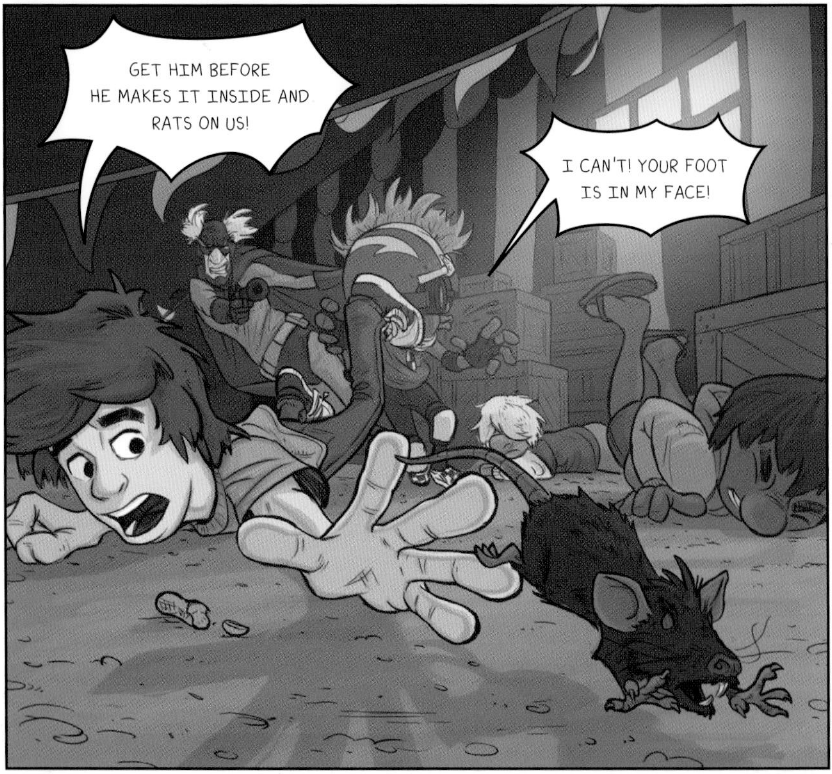
GET HIM BEFORE HE MAKES IT INSIDE AND RATS ON US!
I CAN'T! YOUR FOOT IS IN MY FACE!

Somehow four kids with super powers and a guy with a million super gadgets couldn't catch one tiny mouse! The little critter booked it right back inside, and seconds later, we were face-to-face with The Man With No Name's whole crew!

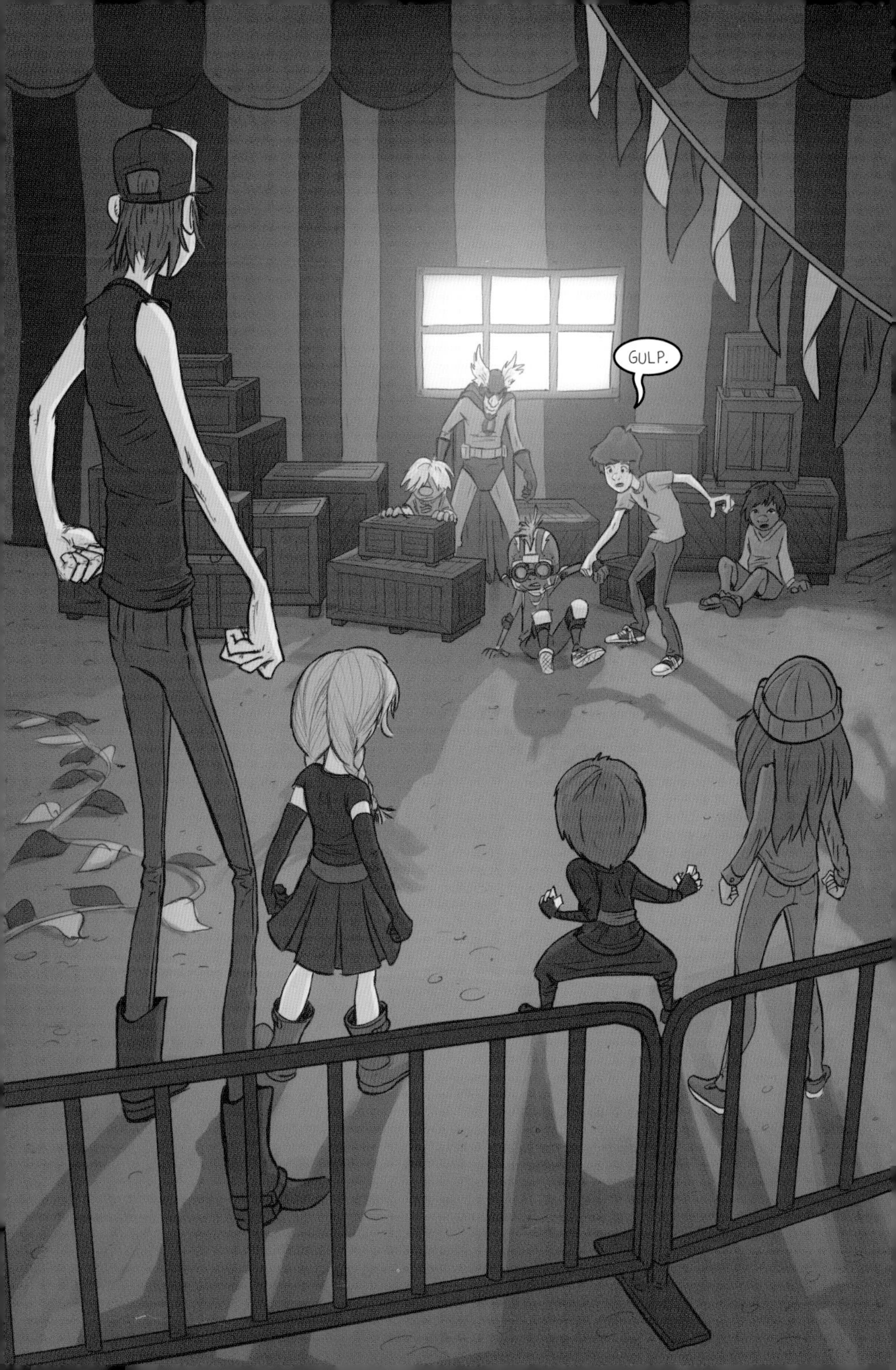
GULP.

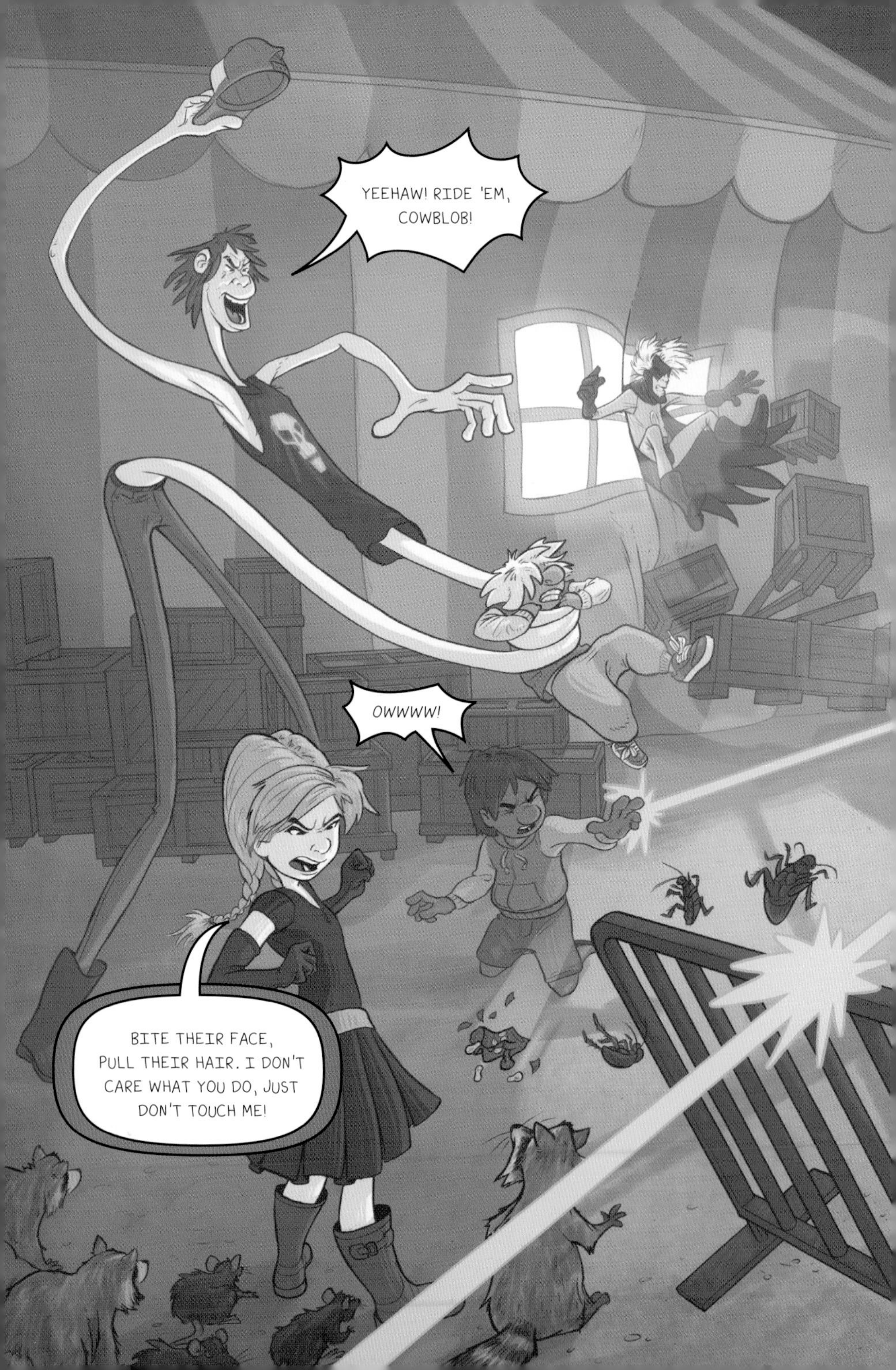
YEEHAW! RIDE 'EM, COWBLOB!
OWWWW!
BITE THEIR FACE, PULL THEIR HAIR. I DON'T CARE WHAT YOU DO, JUST DON'T TOUCH ME!

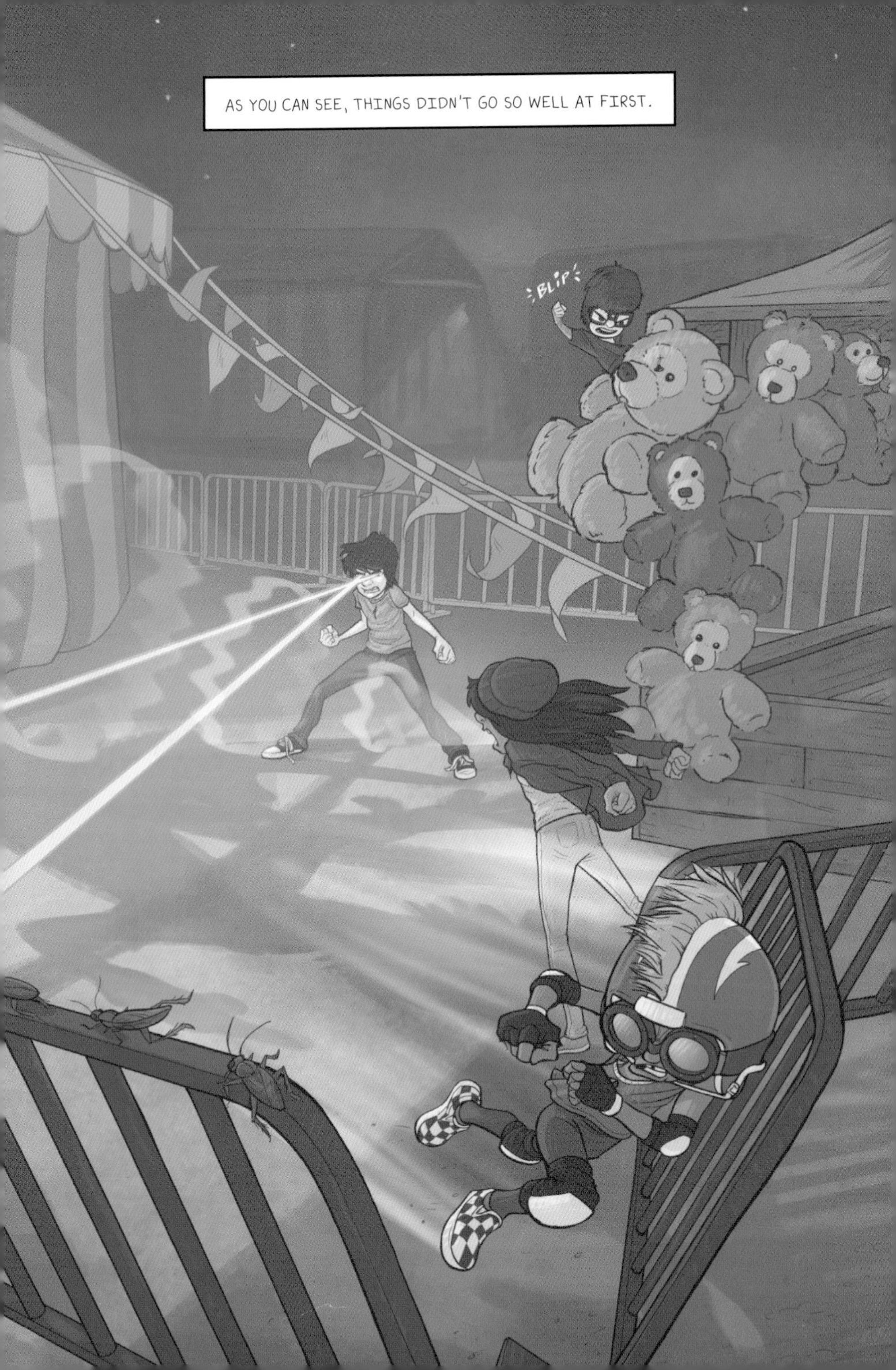
AS YOU CAN SEE, THINGS DIDN'T GO SO WELL AT FIRST.
BLIP

Ninja got a real kick out of blipping away just as Crash charged him.

Thankfully, his blipping backfired on him.

Debbie's pets decided to play keep-away with Tim's peanuts.

Tim played right back. He grabbed one of Debbie's rats and chucked it at a raccoon waiting to catch the bag of peanuts. The bag fell on the ground but was too far for Tim to get to before Debbie's pets did. So Tim stomped on the wooden plank the peanuts were lying on, and the bag went flying over their heads, right into Tim's hands.

I don't think they wanted to play after that.

Meanwhile, The Night Owl threw some smoke bombs to hide from Squeak, but she screamed and blew away the smoke. His next tactic was to hide in the shadows . . .

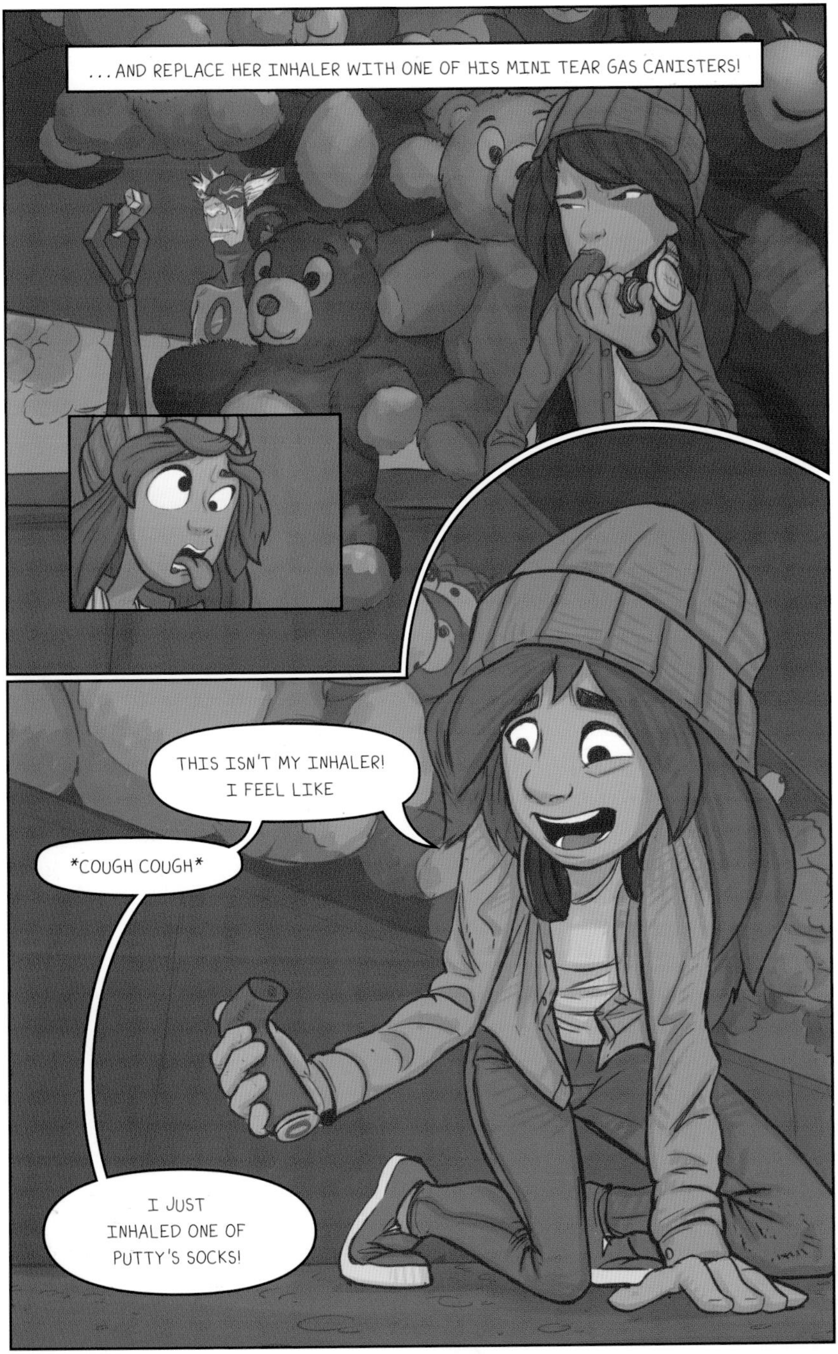
...AND REPLACE HER INHALER WITH ONE OF HIS MINI TEAR GAS CANISTERS!
THIS ISN'T MY INHALER! I FEEL LIKE
COUGH COUGH
I JUST INHALED ONE OF PUTTY'S SOCKS!

Speaking of Putty, I had my hands full with him. I finally tore him off Lewis's face and threw him in a trash can, but he was fighting me so hard I couldn't keep the lid on.

He was starting to take shape again and, of course, the second he got out, he wrapped me in his sweaty arms.

Good thing I had already gone to the bathroom, because Putty squeezed me so hard I almost needed that change of underwear my mom always asks me about.

I don't know what it was with Putty, but he really loved to squeeze people. This was the third time this week he was squeezing me to death, but this time both my hands were trapped so I couldn't twist his arm to make him release me. And Tim was busy going all Jackie Chan on the raccoons, so he wasn't going to save me, either.

I only had a few more seconds before I passed out. So I did something I swore I would never do again.

I flew.

CHAPTER FOURTEEN

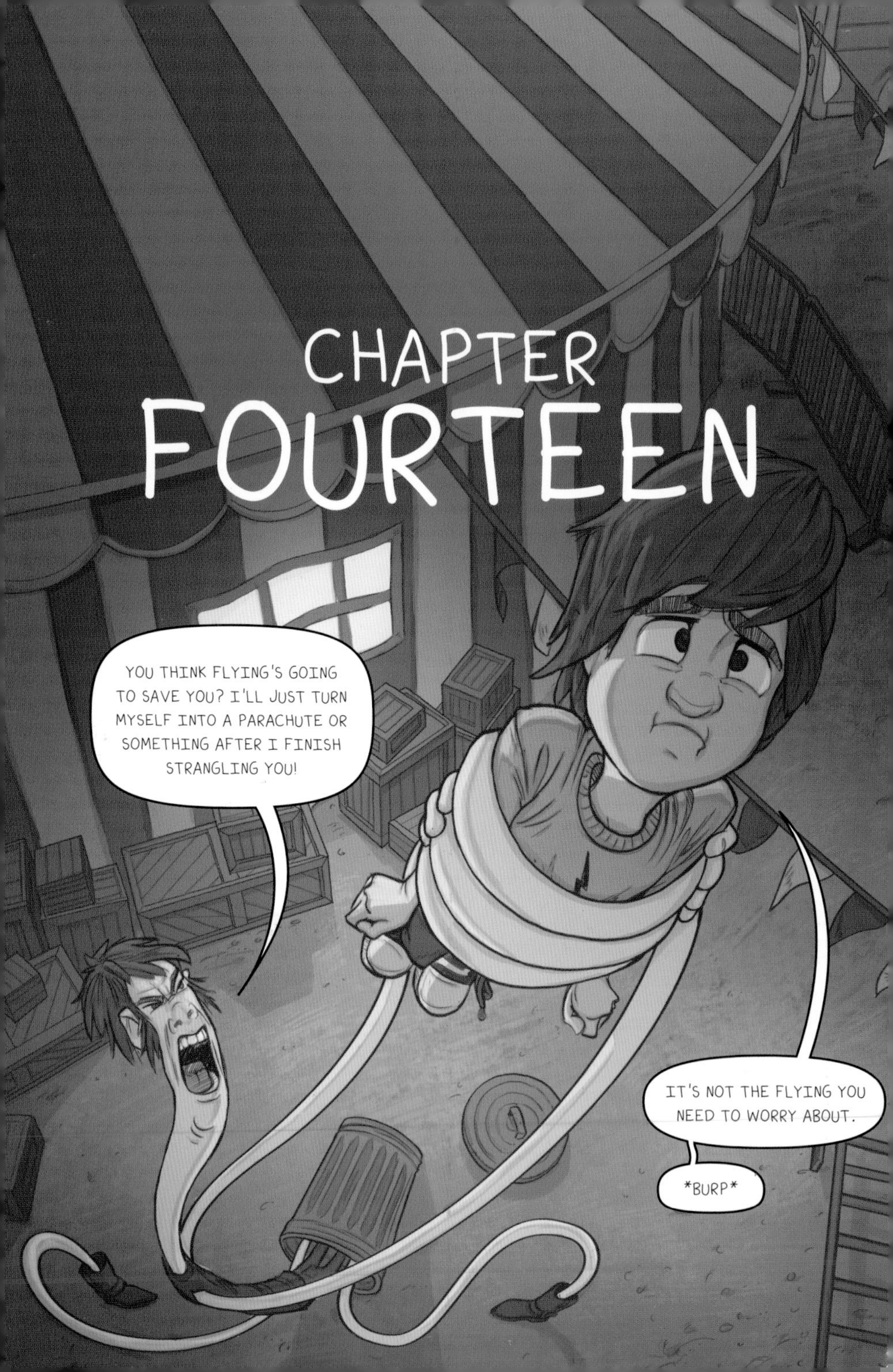
YOU THINK FLYING'S GOING TO SAVE YOU? I'LL JUST TURN MYSELF INTO A PARACHUTE OR SOMETHING AFTER I FINISH STRANGLING YOU!
IT'S NOT THE FLYING YOU NEED TO WORRY ABOUT.
BURP

So, yeah, he let me go after that. And on his way down to the ground, he got a little too close to Squeak, who was still coughing super coughs from the tear gas.

With Squeak, Putty, and Debbie's pet army out of commission, we gathered together at the door and ran inside to confront Mr. Disher, a.k.a. The Man With No Name.

After so many years, The Night Owl was finally face-to-face with his mortal enemy. He leaped up on the desk and grabbed Mr. Disher by the collar. But as he lifted him up, Mr. Disher's chair went with him.

Now why would The Man With No Name be tied to a chair?

But if Mr. Disher wasn't The Man With No Name, then who was?

It was the perfect cover. Trevor must have realized when we came to warn the Superteam about the bomb that he would have to get rid of any evidence back at the school, and Mr. Disher was probably unlucky enough to have been in his classroom when Trevor and his rotten Defective team arrived.

Then his minions hobbled into the arena.

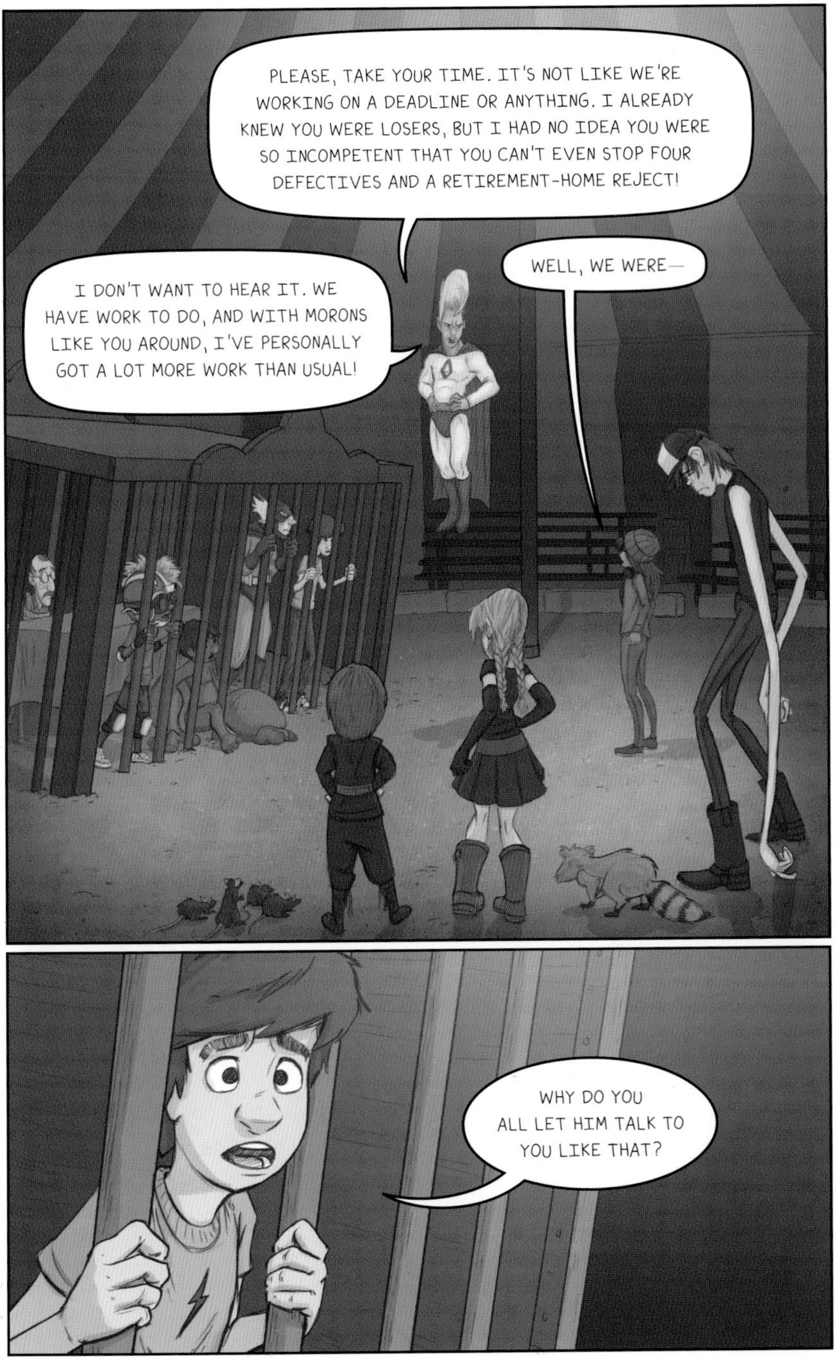
PLEASE, TAKE YOUR TIME. IT'S NOT LIKE WE'RE WORKING ON A DEADLINE OR ANYTHING. I ALREADY KNEW YOU WERE LOSERS, BUT I HAD NO IDEA YOU WERE SO INCOMPETENT THAT YOU CAN'T EVEN STOP FOUR DEFECTIVES AND A RETIREMENT-HOME REJECT!
WELL, WE WERE—
I DON'T WANT TO HEAR IT. WE HAVE WORK TO DO, AND WITH MORONS LIKE YOU AROUND, I'VE PERSONALLY GOT A LOT MORE WORK THAN USUAL!
WHY DO YOU ALL LET HIM TALK TO YOU LIKE THAT?

Then, just like every supervillain does, he revealed his master plan.

The Superteam's security system would detect the bomb if he tried to sneak it in himself, but every building has rats.

Debbie's rats had been sneaking in the bomb, bit by bit, for months. And since Led Zapplin's powers would detect any attempt to detonate it remotely, a few of the hair balls would have to stick around to activate the bomb.

The rats knew their job and were already inside, waiting for 9:15p.m. to roll around.

Squeak, Putty, Debbie, and Ninja all charged Trevor at once. But they're Defectives, and he's a superhero. (Or more like a supervillain, actually.)

Squeak screamed at him with enough force to blow off the back wall, but Trevor stood there like nothing had happened.

THEN HE THREW HER
IN THE CAGE.

Putty attacked with a barrage of punches and kicks, his extended limbs flying, but Trevor dodged them, yawning the whole time. He threw Putty into the cage, too.

Debbie launched every animal she had at him.

Then Trevor faced off with Ninja, who teleported into the cage and jump-kicked Debbie in the back of the head. She yelled at him, and he teleported away ...

Trevor must have figured the Defectives would turn on him once they discovered his real plan, because a bunch of Henchmen, Inc. guys barged into the arena. From what it looked like, they were getting ready to take pictures of the explosion, while Trevor was practicing what he would say in front of the cameras.

After that, Trevor left us to get ready for his performance. He left some henchmen behind to make sure we didn't escape.

You would think with all of our powers combined, it would be really easy for us to get out of a simple cage, but Putty's limbs were already extended when Trevor tied him up, Crash couldn't get a running start, Squeak couldn't catch a breath because of the tear gas, and The Night Owl's equipment kept breaking. I didn't have good enough aim to cut any of the bars. Tim's swelling had already gone back down, and Lewis was, well, Lewis.

But then Ninja teleported back.

NINJA, YOU WONDERFUL LITTLE MUNCHKIN! GET THE KEYS SO WE CAN GET OUT OF HERE!

HE GAVE THE THUMBS-UP AND DISAPPEARED.

And we had no idea where he went, like usual.

WHO IS THIS KID?

WHO CARES?

So we were pretty much on our own.

CHAPTER
FIFTEEN

Knowing Ninja, he was never coming back. Not like it mattered. Even if we could get out of the cage, we couldn't stop the bomb—not with our defective powers. Plus, Debbie told us that the rats sent inside to activate the bomb were on their own; they would do exactly what she had told them to do until they heard her voice again, and there was no way we were going to get to them in time to stop them.

Trevor was probably going to make it look like all of this was our fault. Now that he had us captive, he could blame the whole thing on us, and no one would question him. After all, we were just a bunch of rejects, and he was a town hero and a trusted member of the Superteam.

Just then one of Debbie's rats passed by us. She called to him and sent him to get the keys to the cage, but when he was on his way to bring them to us, he passed a rat trap with peanut butter on it.

He didn't listen.

So our last hope was officially gone.

Or so we thought.

LUCKILY, THERE WAS STILL SOME PEANUT BUTTER ON THE TRAP. EXTRA CHUNKY PEANUT BUTTER!

AT LEAST I *HOPED* IT WAS EXTRA CHUNKY!

Tim didn't look like he wanted to eat it, though. I can't say I blame him. I mean, who knew how long it had been on that trap, not to mention the fact that a rat had just been licking it.

But we had to get out of that cage to stop Trevor and save the Superteam. So we did what all boys do when they find something gross: we dared him to eat it.

DO IT! DO IT! DO IT! DO IT! DO IT! DO IT! DO IT! DO IT! DO IT!

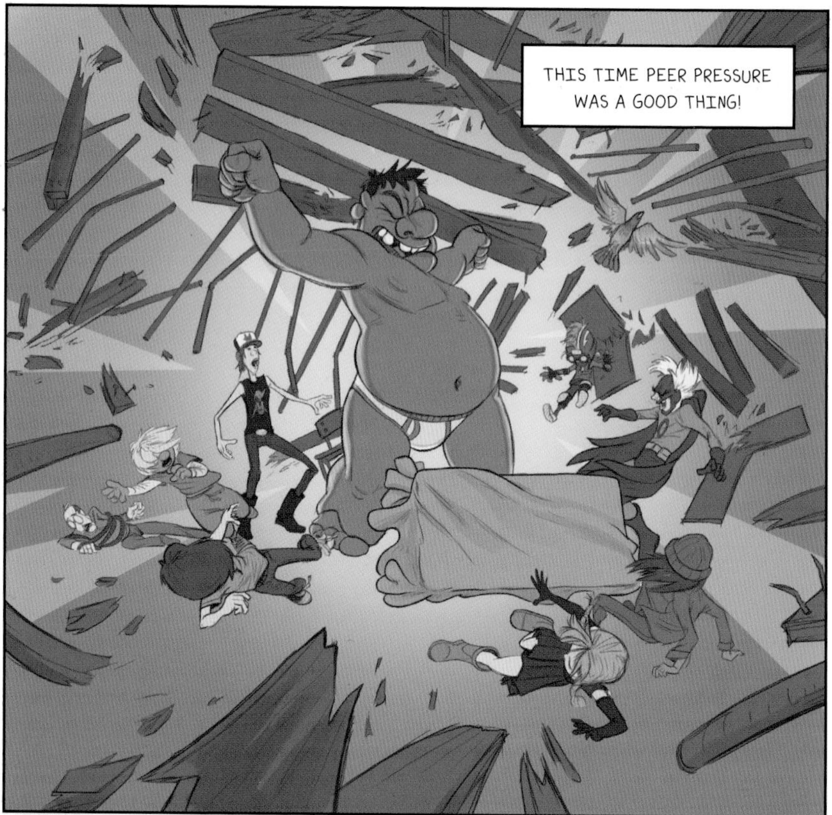
THIS TIME PEER PRESSURE WAS A GOOD THING!

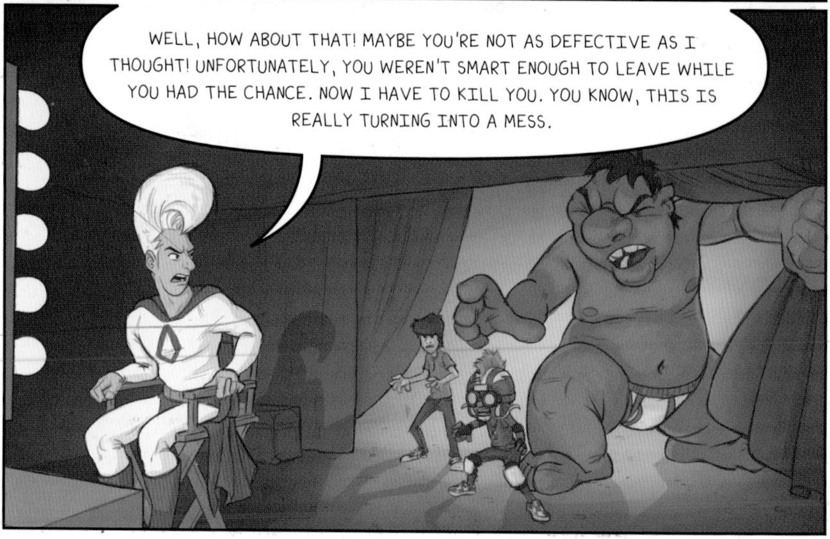
WELL, HOW ABOUT THAT! MAYBE YOU'RE NOT AS DEFECTIVE AS I THOUGHT! UNFORTUNATELY, YOU WEREN'T SMART ENOUGH TO LEAVE WHILE YOU HAD THE CHANCE. NOW I HAVE TO KILL YOU. YOU KNOW, THIS IS REALLY TURNING INTO A MESS.

His henchmen came after us, but we were ready to rumble.

It wasn't easy, but we held our own.

Putty used his limp limbs to take out five of them at one time.

THAT'S GONNA LEAVE A MARK!

Ninja blinked back, and Debbie put the bells from an old carnival costume on a few of the henchmen so Ninja would know who to attack.

AT LEAST HE GOT ONE GUY.

Debbie got into a bit of trouble . . .

. . . until her furry army came to the rescue.

Squeak was doing pretty well until she ran out of breath. One of the henchmen picked her up by the back of the shirt. She punched and kicked, but he was just out of her reach. She didn't have her inhaler, but she did still have The Night Owl's tear gas canister.

Even I was doing awesome. I got a bunch of bad guys to follow me into the Hall of Mirrors.

We kicked some serious henchman butt. And I think we proved that even Defectives can be pretty awesome.

But there was still Trevor.

We ran to help, but The Night Owl locked the door so we couldn't open it.

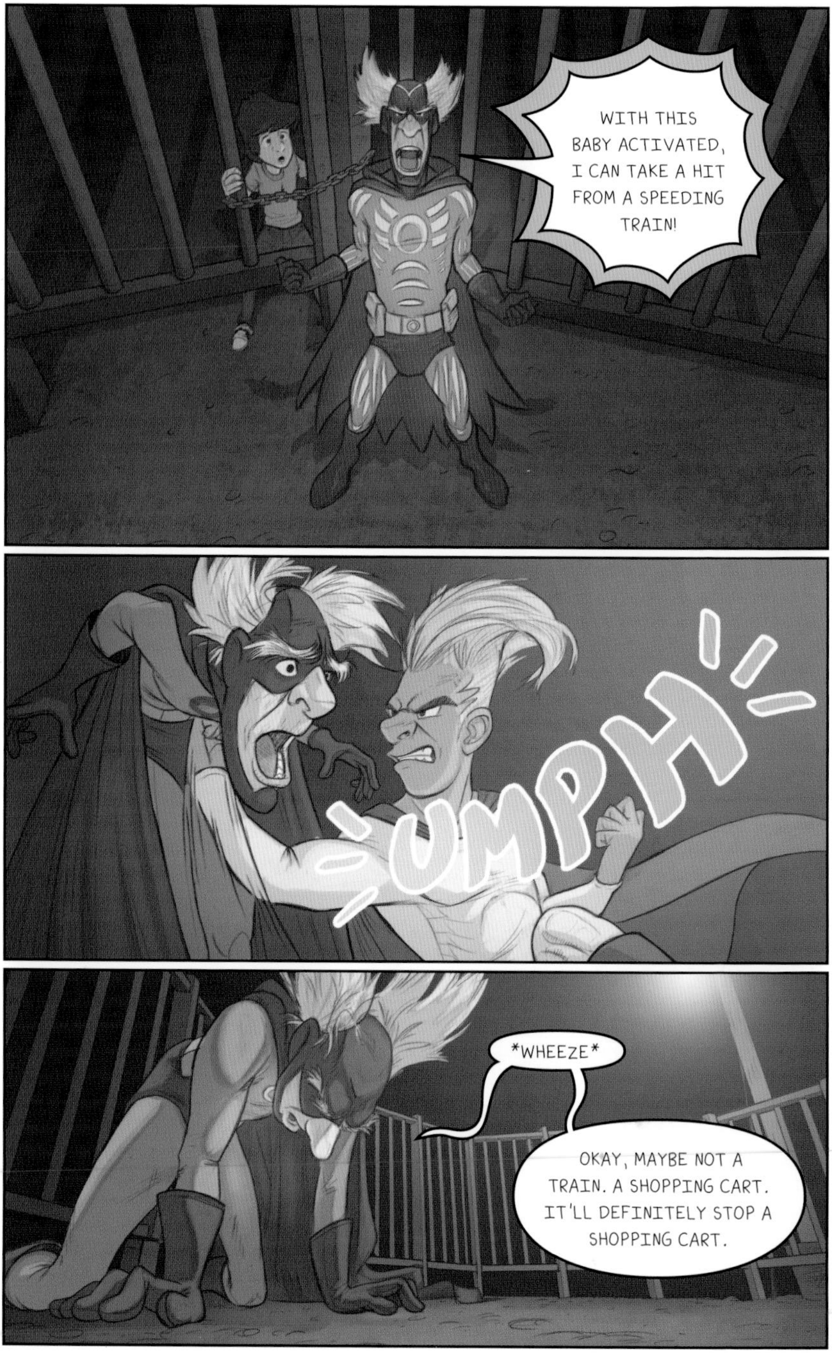
WITH THIS BABY ACTIVATED, I CAN TAKE A HIT FROM A SPEEDING TRAIN!
UMPH
WHEEZE
OKAY, MAYBE NOT A TRAIN. A SHOPPING CART. IT'LL DEFINITELY STOP A SHOPPING CART.

We tried and tried but we couldn't get the door to the cage open. I begged The Night Owl to let us in, but he wouldn't listen.

The Night Owl lied to us! He didn't really believe we could be heroes. If he did, he wouldn't have locked himself in a cage to take on Trevor single-handed. We'd have been fighting Trevor together, like a real team.

Trevor slammed his fist into The Night Owl's stomach and the old man went down, hard.

Just then, Trevor picked him up and threw him so hard, The Night Owl broke out of the cage and slammed into a wall, which came down on top of him. When the dust settled, I could barely see The Night Owl under the rubble. He wasn't moving.

I've got to hand it to them, Squeak and the gang didn't even blink when going up against Trevor, one of the strongest, most powerful superhero-villains I had ever seen.

Squeak's scream caught Trevor off guard. It pushed him back against a wall, if only for a second. That gave Putty time to wrap his arms around Trevor's neck, but that only seemed to annoy him. Then Tim grabbed Trevor in a giant bear hug, but Trevor broke free and slammed Tim through a wall. Crash rammed him headfirst. All that did was rattle

Crash's brain so badly he asked me what time he needed to put his shoes back on. Debbie ordered some raccoons to jump on Trevor's head, which of course did less than nothing since all he had to do was shake them off.

And Ninja ...

... HE GETS AN A FOR EFFORT.

I tried to fire my lasers at Trevor but I didn't even come close to hitting him. And, of course, a piece of metal deflected the beam and it ended up hitting me in the chest.

Things were not looking good for us. Trevor had taken down all of us without even breaking a sweat. We had to stop him, but how? How could a bunch of Defectives hope to defeat a superhero? Had we come this far just to fail?

No way. We couldn't fail. I wouldn't let us. Trevor *couldn't* win. No matter what he said, no matter how he acted or what people thought of him, he wasn't better than us. He was a thousand times worse. He was worse than the kid who crossed his eyes and laughed every time he saw me in the hallway at school; worse than the jerks who would trip me at lunch; worse than the football players who picked on me in the locker room. He was worse than anyone I had ever known, and I was tired of having people worse than me push me around. I wasn't going to take it anymore. Not from anybody. And especially not from Trevor.

So I gritted my teeth and stood between Trevor and my friends.

CHAPTER
SIXTEEN

Going head to head with Trevor was pretty much suicide, but I had to protect my friends.

Trevor thought I was trying to knock him over with my kick, but that wasn't my plan.

He didn't get to finish his sentence.

That got him really mad.

He bear-hugged me, and when he flexed, all the air exploded out of my lungs and my ribs just about snapped in half.

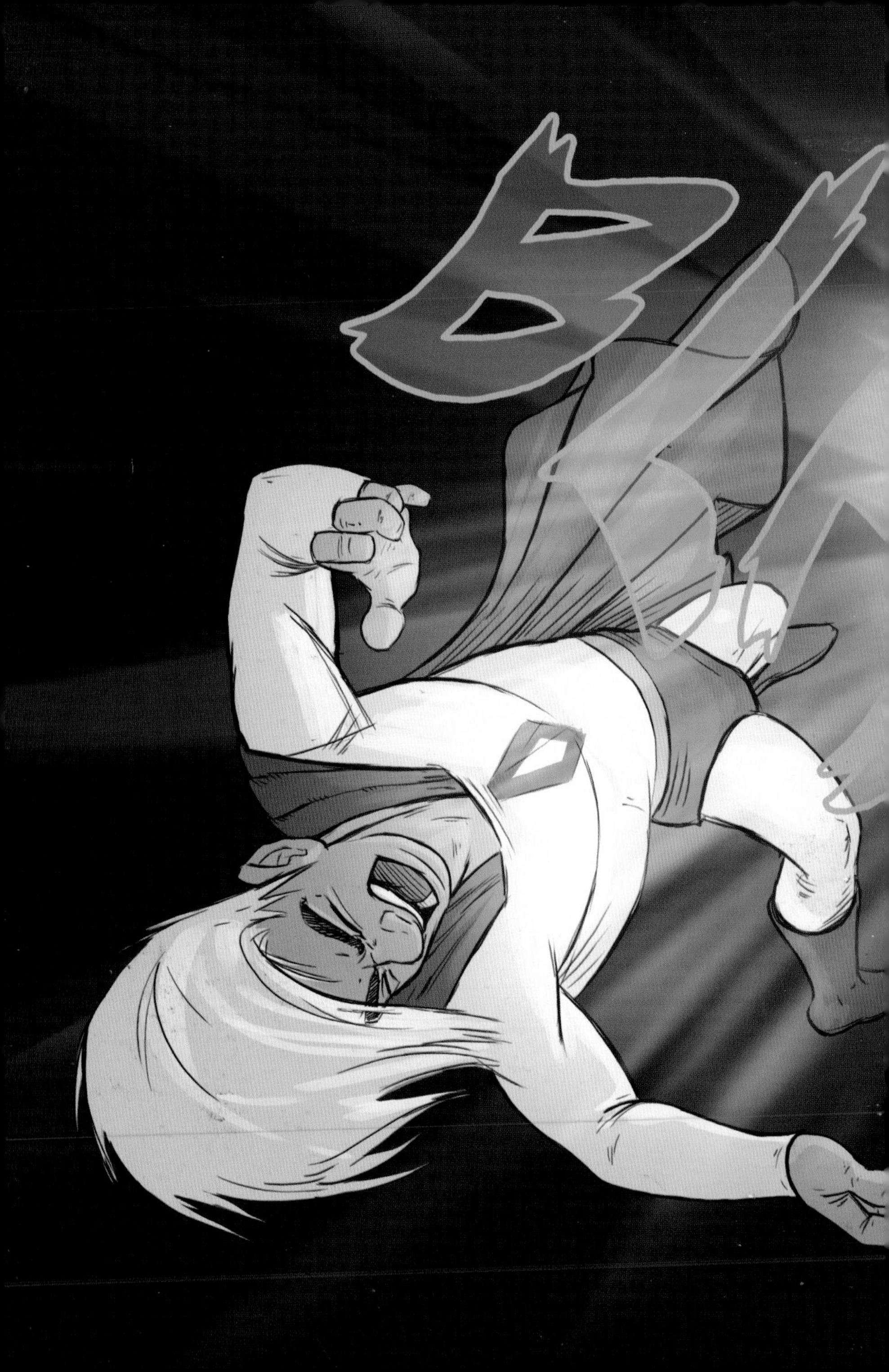

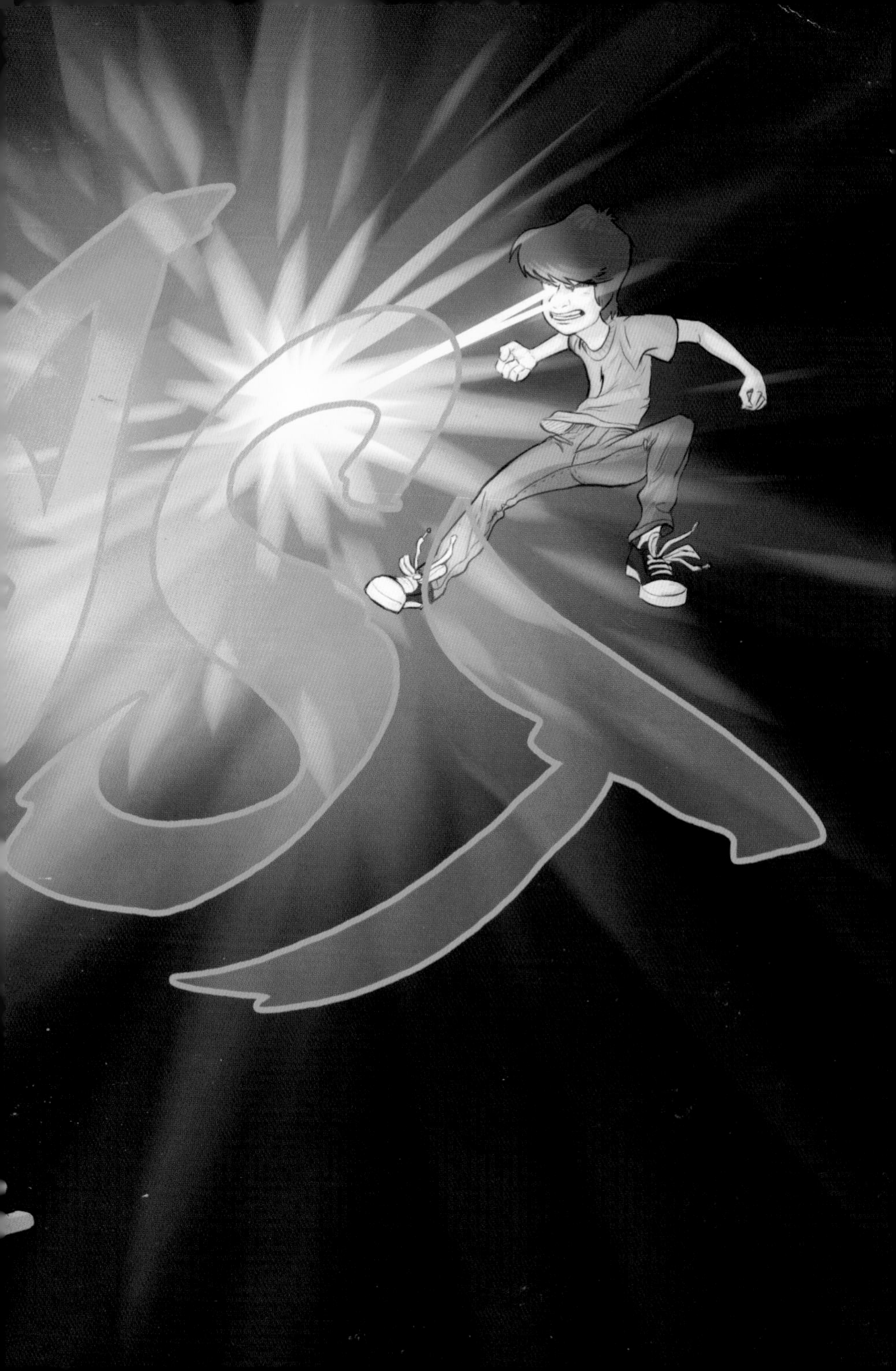

That blast was the biggest I had ever fired in my entire life, and it was a direct hit! It hit Trevor so hard, the wall he ran into fell down on top of him.

That's when The Night Owl crawled out from the rubble.

The Night Owl said The Man With No Name always had a way out, and
Trevor's escape plan was probably set up *exactly* the way he would do it.
After all, Trevor wouldn't want to blow his cover.

The Night Owl was right about the tower, but Trevor had given the rats very specific orders. If the wrong tower lights were turned on, the bomb would go off early.

Trevor said that when he studied The Man With No Name, he learned about his nemesis, The Night Owl, and that when The Night Owl lost his sidekick, it had nearly destroyed him.

I had no idea what we were going to do.

But The Night Owl did.

We did it! We had rescued the best superhero team in the world from being blown to pieces! We stopped the bomb from going off, we finally found The Man With No Name, and I even got to blast Trevor with my lasers!

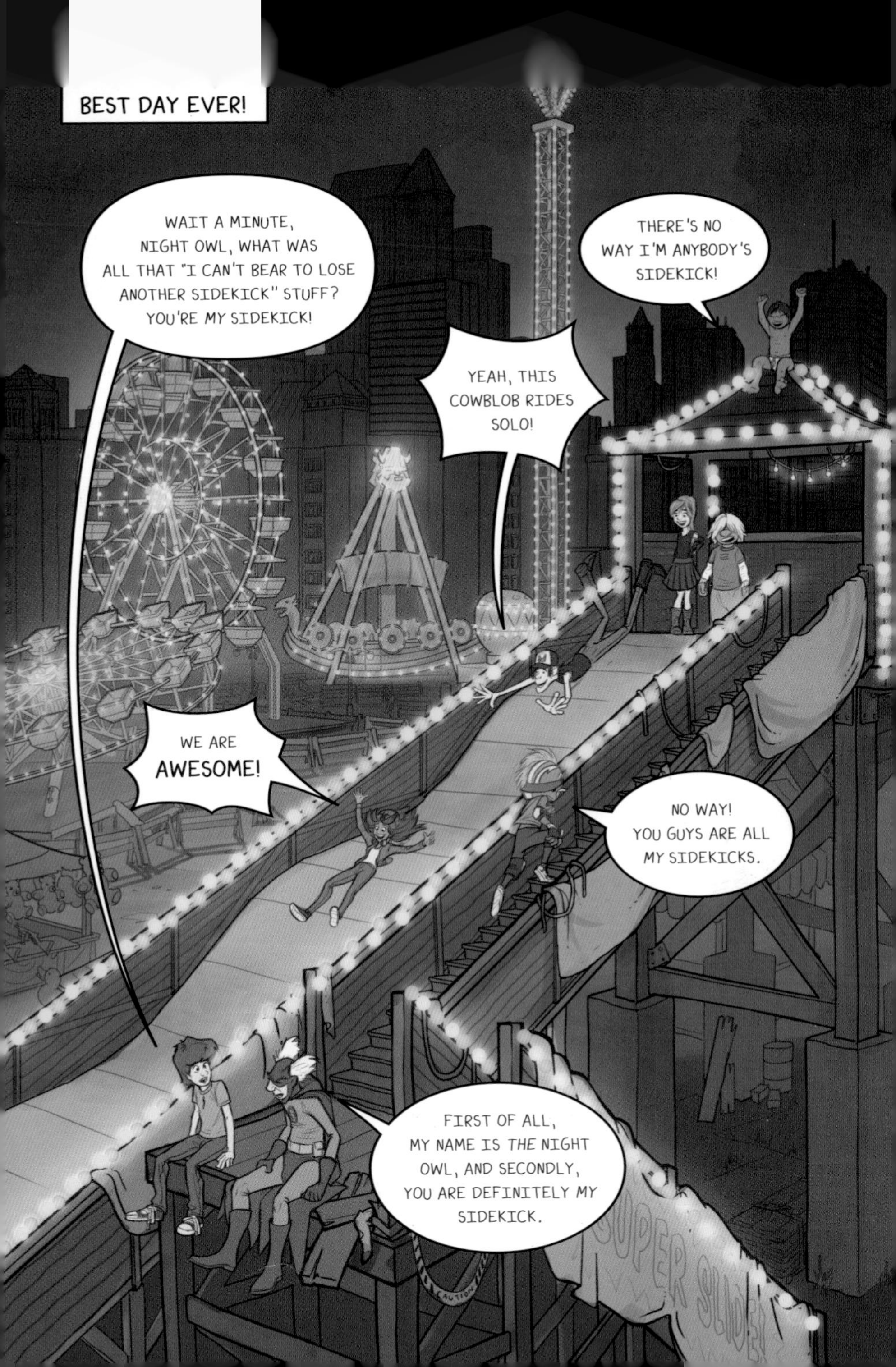
BEST DAY EVER!
WAIT A MINUTE, NIGHT OWL, WHAT WAS ALL THAT "I CAN'T BEAR TO LOSE ANOTHER SIDEKICK" STUFF? YOU'RE MY SIDEKICK!
THERE'S NO WAY I'M ANYBODY'S SIDEKICK!
YEAH, THIS COWBLOB RIDES SOLO!
WE ARE AWESOME!
NO WAY! YOU GUYS ARE ALL MY SIDEKICKS.
FIRST OF ALL, MY NAME IS *THE* NIGHT OWL, AND SECONDLY, YOU ARE DEFINITELY MY SIDEKICK.
SUPER SLIDE
CAUTION

CHAPTER SEVENTEEN

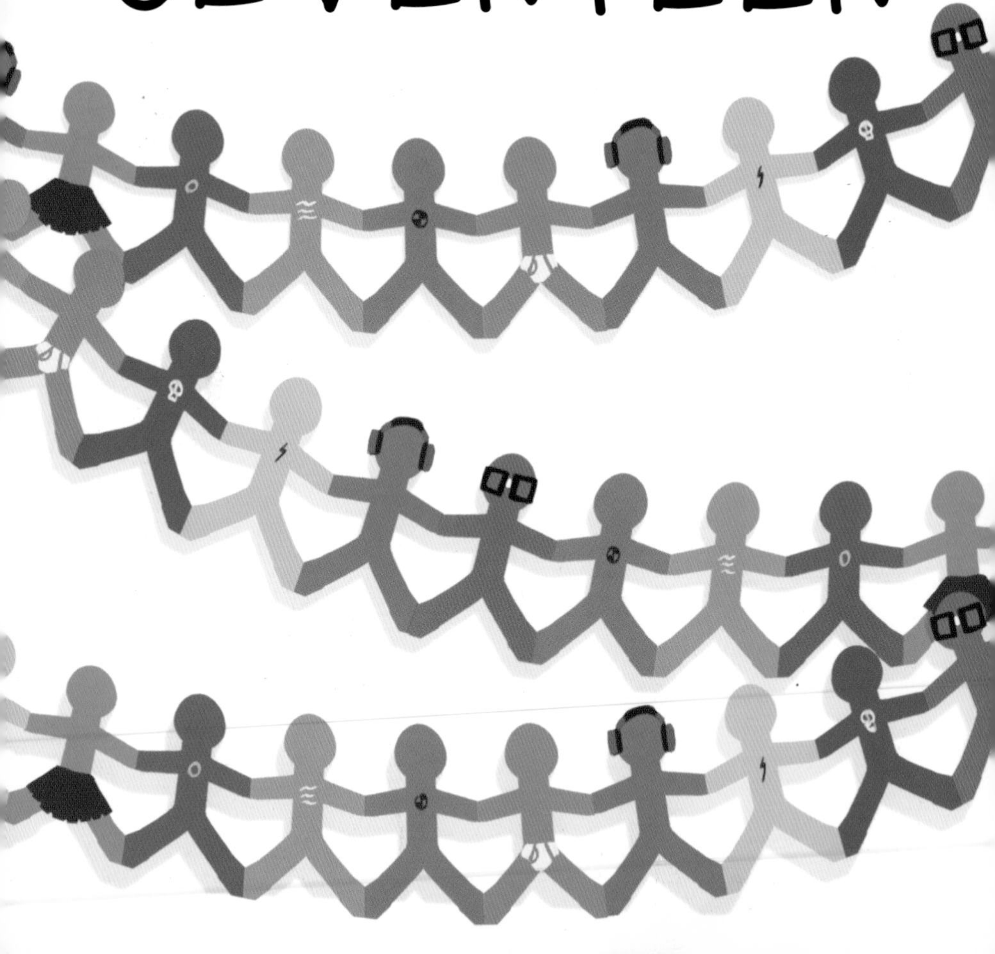

After things calmed down, I called the Superteam and they arrested Trevor. Even they had to admit we did an awesome job.

Finally, we were the heroes! TV crews came to cover the Superteam's unveiling of their new wing, but they turned their cameras on us instead. We were on TV! Like celebrities!

I've got to tell you, it felt pretty good to finally be the hero.

The Night Owl smiled and put his hand on my shoulder.

I took off my glasses, looked right into the camera, and said:

NEWS
NEWS

SUNNYVILLE TIMES

DAILY NEWS
DAILY NEWS
DAILY NEWS

.34 SUNNYVILLE, ILLINOIS, FRIDAY, AUGUST 8, 2017 A1

THE DEFECTIVES

A SUPERHERO TEAM THAT'S NOT SO SUPER

The newest kids on the block. They may have powers like laser vision, super speed, and teleportation, but this team of heroes is anything but ordinary. Laser vision is tough to control when you're cross-eyed. Super speed

Despite their defective super powers, this team managed to thwart a plot to eliminate the greatest superhero team our city has ever known: The Superteam. That's right, these Defective kids saved the Superteam. Pairing

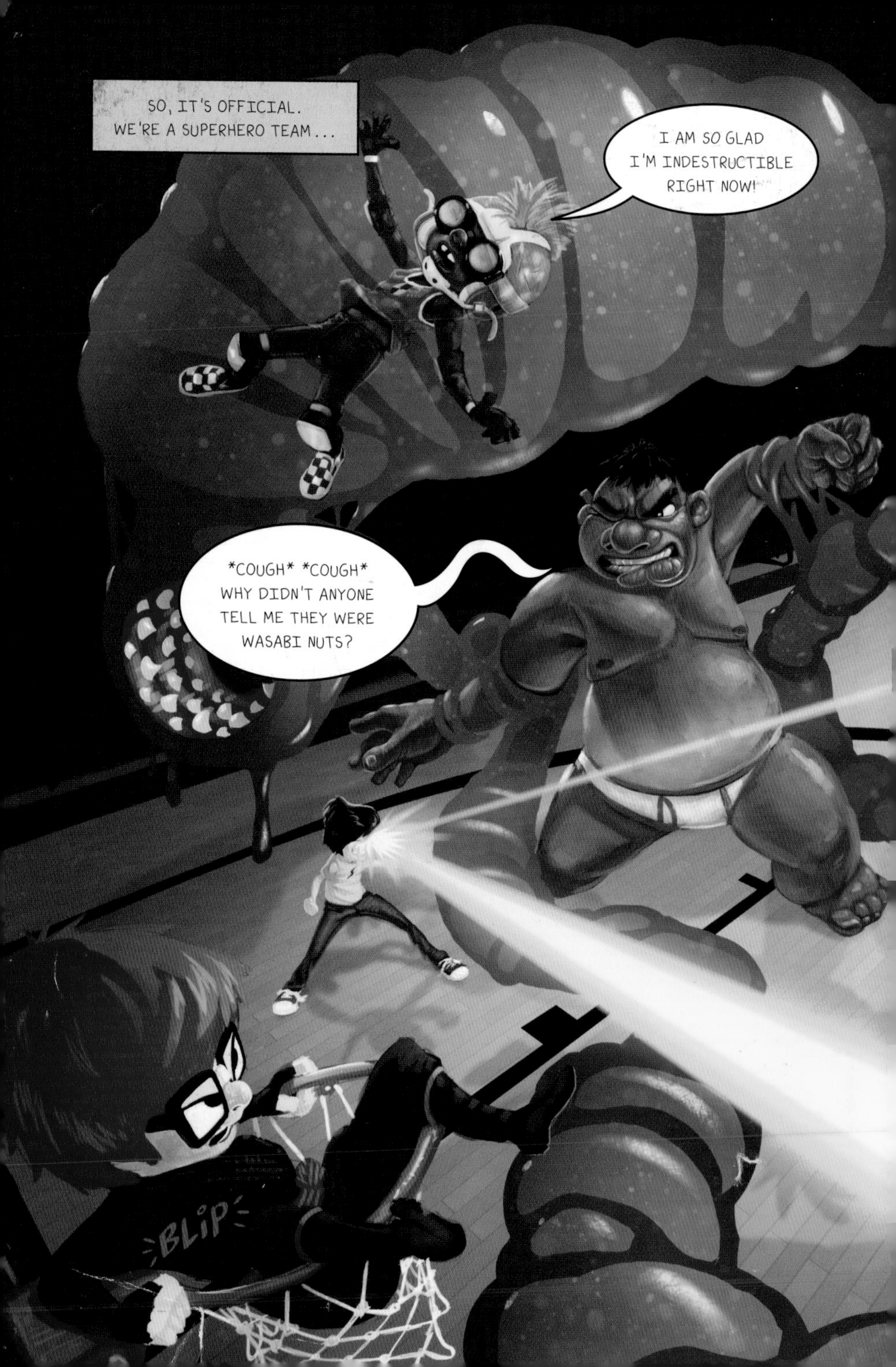
SO, IT'S OFFICIAL. WE'RE A SUPERHERO TEAM...
I AM SO GLAD I'M INDESTRUCTIBLE RIGHT NOW!
COUGH *COUGH* WHY DIDN'T ANYONE TELL ME THEY WERE WASABI NUTS?
BLIP

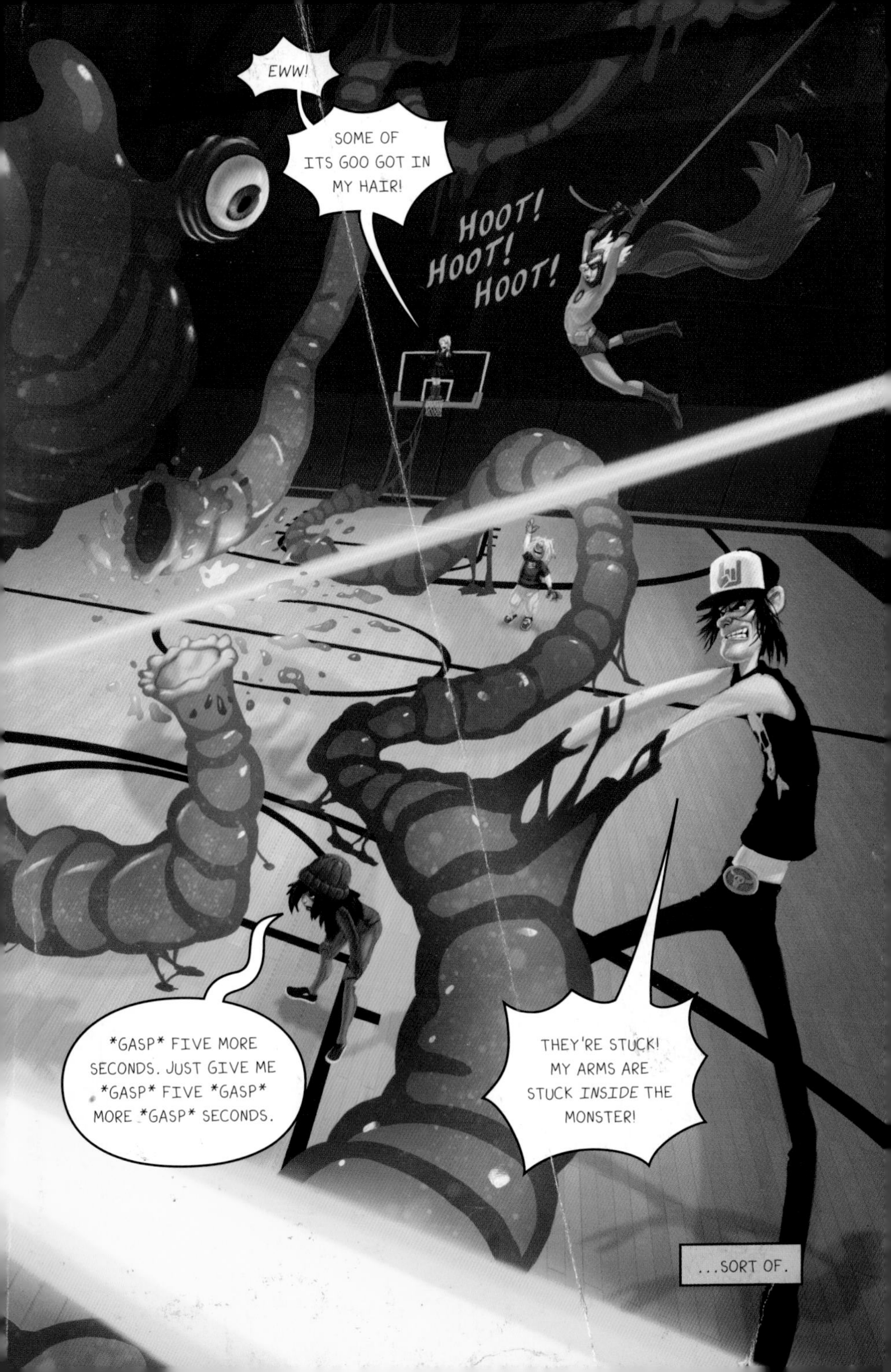
EWW!
SOME OF ITS GOO GOT IN MY HAIR!
HOOT! HOOT! HOOT!
GASP FIVE MORE SECONDS. JUST GIVE ME *GASP* FIVE *GASP* MORE *GASP* SECONDS.
THEY'RE STUCK! MY ARMS ARE STUCK *INSIDE* THE MONSTER!
...SORT OF.

ACKNOWLEDGMENTS

I owe a very special thanks to my sweet, patient, long-suffering (not to mention gorgeous) wife. Thank you for putting up with so many lonely nights while I wrote until sunrise. Even as I write this acknowledgment, you wait for me to finish without complaint, giving of yourself to support my ambitions. Thank you for being who you are, for your love, and for your constant encouragement. Without you, this book would still be a half-written document collecting digital dust on our computer. Thank you for being my strength.

Amanda Reschke has been instrumental in shaping this book. *Superfail* would not be half of what it is without her expertise, her skills, and her invaluable insights. Thank you for the countless hours you spent working on one of my hair-brained ideas. Your influence can truly be felt on every page.

I cannot express how thankful I am for our agent and number-one fan, Clelia Gore. Rejection after rejection, she believed in *Superfail* and in what it represents. Thank you for never giving up on Marshall and his friend, for making sure that *Superfail* found the right home, and for continuing to be our champion.

I will be forever grateful to my incredible, ever-faithful parents and their unwavering encouragement and wisdom. To them and to my loving and supportive family and friends, I thank you for believing in me even when I didn't even believe in myself. You have all played a special part in making this book into a reality and in making my dreams come true.

—M.B.

Ash, Pen, Roo, and baby goof—I, like this book, belong to you.

—D.M.

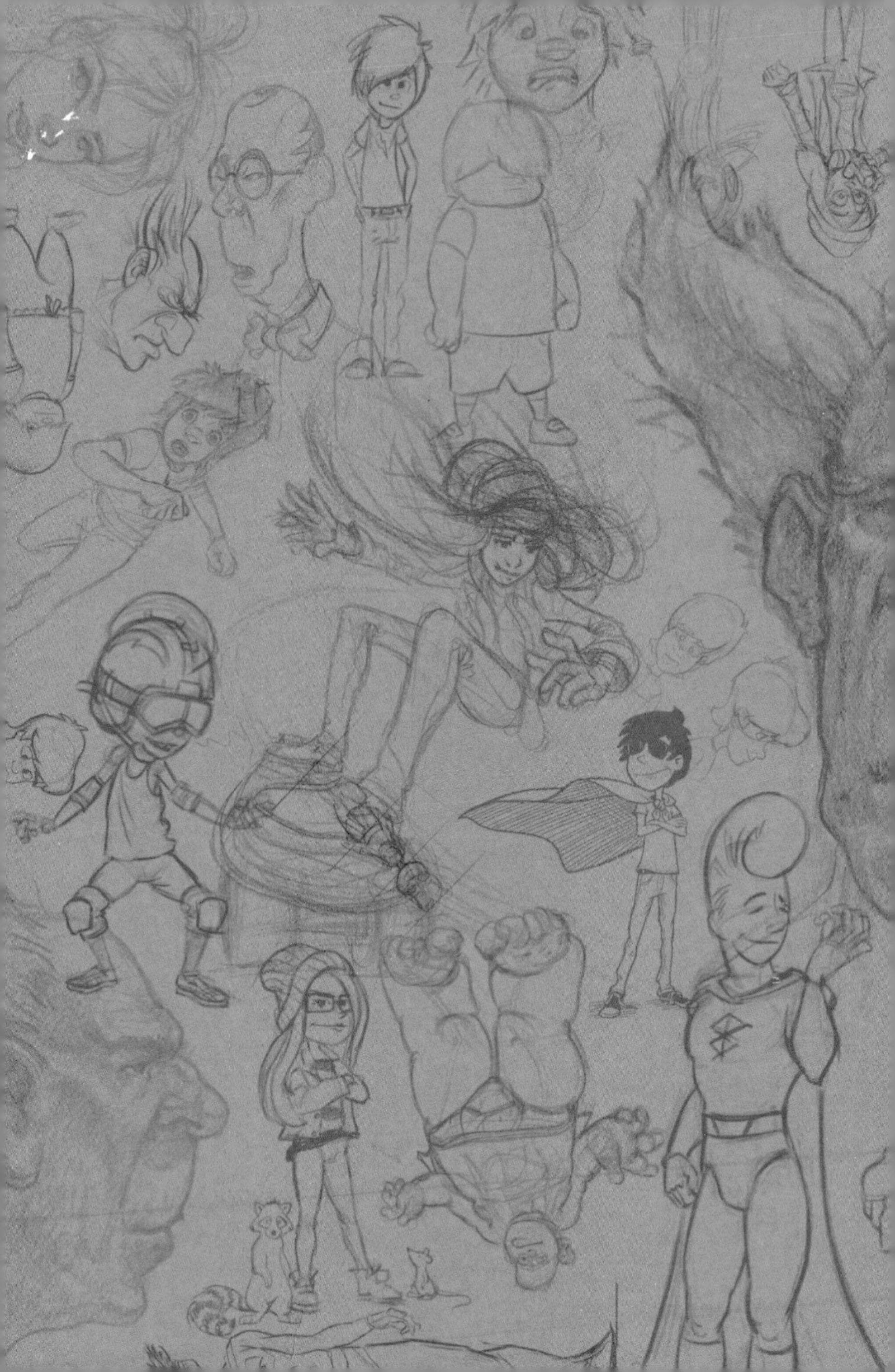